Brandon had known somehow the little girl was his as soon as he'd looked into her eyes and seen the same dark green as his own.

Lacey had lied to him—for five years. And made him a man worse than his father.

He had never planned to have children. Never even contemplated it. For the simple reason he was fairly sure he did not have the sensibilities to nurture or protect a child. But it was way too late to worry about that now.

He had to deal with what was, not what should have been.

Ruby Devlin Carstairs was a part of him. And however angry he was with her mother for keeping her existence from him, however angry he was with himself for not checking on Lacey after that long-ago encounter, he could not abandon the child... The way his own mother had abandoned him.

How the hell he was going to form a relationship with this child, he had no idea. He knew absolutely nothing about children. But one thing was certain—her mother would no longer be calling the shots.

USA TODAY bestselling author **Heidi Rice** lives in London, England. She is married with two teenage sons—which gives her rather too much of an insight into the male psyche—and also works as a film journalist. She adores her job, which involves getting swept up in a world of high emotions; sensual excitement; funny, feisty women; sexy, tortured men; and glamorous locations where laundry doesn't exist. Once she turns off her computer, she often does chores—usually involving laundry!

Books by Heidi Rice

Harlequin Presents

Banished Prince to Desert Boss

Billion-Dollar Christmas Confessions
Unwrapping His New York Innocent

Hot Summer Nights with a Billionaire
One Wild Night with Her Enemy

Passionately Ever After...
A Baby to Tame the Wolfe

Secrets of Billionaire Siblings
The Billionaire's Proposition in Paris
The CEO's Impossible Heir

Visit the Author Profile page
at Harlequin.com for more titles.

Heidi Rice

REVEALING HER BEST KEPT SECRET

HARLEQUIN

PRESENTS

ISBN-13: 978-1-335-73904-9

Revealing Her Best Kept Secret

Copyright © 2023 by Heidi Rice

Harlequin Enterprises ULC
22 Adelaide St. West, 41st Floor
Toronto, Ontario M5H 4E3, Canada
www.Harlequin.com

Printed in U.S.A.

REVEALING HER BEST KEPT SECRET

To Rob, my hero.

CHAPTER ONE

Do NOT PANIC. There's no way on earth Brandon Cade will remember you.

Lacey Carstairs recited the mantra for the fiftieth time. Unfortunately, it was doing nothing to steady her galloping heartbeat or reduce the boiling pain in her temples at the thought of the interview which loomed large in her future with the man who had ground her heart—and her career prospects—to dust beneath the heel of his hand-made Italian leather loafers.

'Do you know how much longer Mr Cade is likely to be?' Lacey asked the receptionist in the stark and stylish penthouse offices of Cade Tower on London's South Bank.

'This interview is not his top priority today,' the woman replied, with enough haughty superiority to put Lacey firmly in her place. 'But he should be with you soon. He has a meeting scheduled in Paris in…' she clicked on her tablet '…two hours.'

'Two hours, but surely…?' Lacey trailed off, her anxiety catching up with her reporter's instincts.

Cade's tight schedule could be a bonus. Surely he would have to reschedule? It took longer than two hours to get to Paris from here.

'We have a heliport on the roof,' the receptionist replied, crushing that hope like a bug. 'He won't have to leave till two.'

Fabulous. 'Right.'

So, no reprieve. But the good news was he had less than an hour now before he had to leave, so the interview would have to be brief—a reprieve of sorts.

Her gaze strayed to the glass wall behind the receptionist's desk, and the sky-high view of the Thames snaking lazily past the steel-and-glass blocks of London's Square Mile, the City's financial hotspot.

How fitting that the most powerful media mogul in Europe should conduct his empire from the top of the continent's tallest building. Unfortunately, the bubble of vertigo wasn't doing much for the nausea lying low in Lacey's stomach.

The thought of having to see Brandon Cade again had kept her up all night. So she now had the foggy feeling of exhaustion to add to the double whammy of terror and stress which had slammed into her yesterday evening, when her editor, Melody, had phoned with the 'stupendous news'—Lacey would be handling the Cade profile because Tiffany Bradford, the magazine's star feature writer, had flu.

Unless Lacey wanted to kill her career a second time—and/or come up with a viable explanation as to why she was the only female magazine journalist in the known universe who would rather shoot herself in the head than spend sixty minutes with the world's handsomest and most dynamic billionaire bachelor. Refusing simply hadn't been an option.

Not that Melody had given her an option.

This interview was a seriously big deal for *Splendour* magazine. It had been three months in the offing, the result of intense negotiations between the magazine's executive editor and the might of Cade Inc's PR department. Even so, Lacey had no doubt at all Brandon Cade would have refused, but for the media furore surrounding his ex-mistress's kiss-and-tell book, which was currently threatening to derail the company's acquisition plans in the US.

Misty Goodnight had painted an evocative portrait of an impossibly handsome, powerful, sexually dominant and yet wholly unknowable autocrat of thirty-one, who treated his women with the same cool, calm, ruthless detachment with which he ran the empire he had inherited from his father at seventeen.

Lacey happened to know Misty hadn't lied—or rather, her army of ghost writers hadn't lied. The tabloid press had taken the story and run with it, dubbing Cade 'the Great Gasp-by', thanks to Misty's lurid depictions of his sexual prowess.

Lacey's nipples drew into hard peaks at the visceral memory of her one time with Cade. She swallowed down the aching pain in her throat and crossed her arms over her swollen breasts.

Don't go there. Do not go there. Ever.

The evidence Cade still had a sexual hold on her

body after one thirty-minute encounter five years ago was as mortifying as it was disturbing.

He will not remember you.

She repeated the mantra to quell the rising tide of hysteria.

He would never put the smart, sophisticated, perfectly styled magazine journalist together with the eager-to-please intern he had once seduced. She'd changed her name, cut her hair down from long chestnut waves to a curly bob, lost nearly ten pounds—thanks so much, Ruby and her terrible twos—and changed her wardrobe from the second-hand clothes she'd once kidded herself were vintage to the chic lines of the designer labels that were just within her reach now, if she budgeted accordingly.

But, most of all, she'd got a lot less stupid in the intervening years. He'd destroyed her, simply because he could. He'd seduced her at the Carrell launch party and had then napalmed her career. She still hadn't quite figured out why he'd had her sacked. It wasn't as if she'd made any demands of him, or expected anything after that mind-blowing encounter. Perhaps she should add paranoid and vindictive to his list of character flaws.

He doesn't need to know about Ruby.

The familiar guilt pricked her conscience.

Maybe one day, if her daughter wanted to know who her biological father was, she could tell her. But, until that day came, Lacey refused to throw herself or her daughter on Brandon Cade's mercy. Given the ruthless way he'd treated her once, she didn't hold out much hope of his reaction to an illegitimate child being good, or even rational.

And she would never subject a child to a father like her own.

She bit into her lip. Tasted the tiny hint of metal to remind herself not to get carried away.

You're not scared or heartbroken any more, like that starry-eyed nineteen-year-old. You're cool, aloof and indifferent now. Just like him.

Brandon Cade was even on record as saying he didn't want children. So why would she tell him about Ruby?

Thank goodness Cade's PR team had insisted any discussion of his private life was out of bounds. Of course, Melody had implied a good feature writer ignored those kinds of rules. Well, not Lacey. Not this time.

The musical chime of the receptionist's smartphone startled her.

'Yes, I'll send her up, then.' The receptionist clicked off her phone. 'If you'd like to take the lift to the top floor, Mr Cade's EA will be waiting for you.'

Lacey crossed the lobby with as much purpose in her stride as she could muster to step into the scenic lift. The panoramic view of metal and glass across the water glittered like jewels in the noon sunshine. She pressed the top floor button. The buildings dropped away while the writhing snakes in the pit of her stomach plummeted to her toes.

You have nothing whatsoever to worry about. No way on earth will Brandon Cade remember the likes of you.

CHAPTER TWO

BRANDON CADE STARED at the muddy brown line of the River Thames eighty-five floors below him. He drew in a tight breath, his nostrils flaring as he counted out on the exhale. He'd taught himself the breathing technique in childhood to stop himself from crying—and eventually from showing any emotion at all—at his first boarding school, age five. The technique had also come in useful to help him control his anxiety on the rare occasions when he'd come face to face with his father. But as he waited for his assistant to usher in the feature writer from *Splendour* magazine it was the first time he'd had to use it in years, to maintain the icy demeanour he was famous for.

He never talked to the damn press—ironic, when one considered Cade Inc owned ten global newspaper titles, a raft of cable and digital broadcasters in the UK and Europe and was currently in negotiations to acquire a media conglomerate in North America. But Cade Inc's brand was all about hard news. He didn't own any lifestyle magazines and had no social media interests for the simple reason he despised the kind of powder-puff journalism glossy magazines such as *Splendour* peddled to the masses.

And now, thanks to his affair with a woman who had bored him in bed after approximately ten minutes, he found himself in a straitjacket of his own making. The intrusion infuriated him.

He was suing Misty, of course, and given the expertise of his legal team, and the might of the media empire he controlled, he knew her memoir of their not-at-all memorable sexual exploits would never reach the shelves. But enough of it had been leaked online to make his negotiating team concerned about finalising the deal to acquire the very conservative Dixon Media Group in Atlanta. Hence the need for this damage limitation exercise.

Next time, maybe don't date social media influencers who are as shrewd and ruthless as you are.

'Mr Cade, Ms Carstairs from *Splendour* magazine is here, shall I show her in?' Daryl, his executive assistant, announced.

Brandon unclenched his jaw and took another careful breath. 'Sure.'

He turned from the window, thrusting clenched fists into the pockets of his suit trousers. But as the woman stepped into the office behind his EA, her slim figure accentuated by a demure power suit and her head bent, a bizarre thing happened. A ripple of reaction streaked down his spine, and his senses, which had been jaded ever since a torrid encounter with a very different woman during a company event five years ago roared back to life.

His gaze narrowed on the short cap of wavy curls, the lightning strike of awareness firing through his system as irritating as it was unexpected.

'Ms Carstairs, Mr Cade,' Daryl announced, showing Brandon's unwanted guest into the large airy office. 'You have exactly twenty minutes before Mr Cade has to depart for Paris, Ms Carstairs,' he added. 'Would you like anything to drink?'

'No, thank you,' the woman replied, her voice a smoky purr, which tugged at Brandon's memory and did not help one bit with the inexplicable reaction. The slight tremble in her tone and the way her fingers clutched her bag in a death grip suggested she was nervous.

Good—she ought to be. He didn't want her here. But then she crossed the room and he caught a lungful of her scent—citrus and spice, and as annoyingly intoxicating as the rest of her.

His jaw tensed as visceral heat pounded into his groin.

Great. Was he actually getting turned on?

As if it wasn't bad enough he was having to speak to this journalist, he noticed the tempting glimpse of cleavage peeking from the vee of her blue silk blouse, and the toned legs accentuated by her pencil skirt. He shook his head to dispel the vivid image of his tanned hand cupping the pale swell of her breast, the mouth-watering thought of her nipple elongating against his tongue…

'Take a seat, Ms Carstairs,' he said sharply as Daryl left the room. 'What is your first name?' he asked, surprised to realise he was curious. He wanted to see her face, to gauge her reaction to him—because he felt at a disadvantage, and he didn't like it.

The brusque enquiry did the trick. At last, her head rose and she looked directly at him. But only for a second. That single glimpse was enough for him to make several important observations, though.

Her eyes were a fathomless chocolate-brown with hints of amber, and had a similarly slanted cat-like shape as those of the girl he remembered. And had tried very hard to forget. He'd never seen the colour of that girl's eyes. It had been too dark in the club and the empty manager's office where they'd ended up making love—or rather having raw, frantic, sweaty sex over a desk. But he still remembered the shape of her cheek in the moonlight, the tilt of her eyelashes, and could still hear the sound of her broken sobs as she'd climaxed.

Stop thinking about her, dammit.

He forced his mind away from the unsettling memory. And concentrated on the other thing he'd seen in this woman's eyes.

Awareness. Wary and guarded, but there none the less. Apparently, she was attracted to him too…but was equally as unhappy about it.

Unusual. When was the last time a woman had desired him and not been eager to follow through on it? Her novel reaction made the need surge.

'Lacey,' she said, and he heard the tremble of nerves again. 'Lacey Carstairs.'

She took the seat he'd indicated, brushing her skirt over her lush backside to sit.

Is she doing that deliberately?

But then her knuckles whitened on her smartphone as she retrieved it from her purse. She wasn't just nervous, she looked scared, as if she would rather be anywhere else but in his office—with him—despite the mutual flare of attraction.

Interesting.

She had to know he was giving this interview under duress, and if she had done her research she would also know he wasn't a good man to cross. If someone displeased or threatened him, he acted swiftly and without mercy. Just ask that artless girl who had lured him in and sacrificed her virginity, believing their rare sexual chemistry could be bartered for something more.

He frowned, aware he was thinking of that girl again whom he'd exorcised from his consciousness five years ago.

'Do you mind if I record this, Mr Cade?' the journalist asked, engaging the voice app on her phone with shaking fingers.

'Go ahead, Lacey,' he said, pleased when the use of her given name made her stiffen.

Of course, he had no intention of allowing anything to go into print he hadn't agreed to. One of the stipulations his PR team had insisted on was that he would have final approval on the article before it went to press. And he would also demand any notes or tapes be destroyed as a matter of course. But, even so, he didn't usually allow his words to be recorded.

'And please call me Brandon,' he added.

As expected, the offer had her head jerking up. This time, their gazes locked and held. The surge of heat crackled in the air between them. But he was prepared for it now. Enough to find himself enjoying the flare of reaction lighting the gold shards in the rich brown of her irises and flushing her pale skin a vivid pink.

Yes, she could feel it too, this rare electric chemistry. But what had unnerved him five years ago with that girl excited him now. His sex life had been non-existent since the Misty debacle, and had lacked the visceral spark of attraction for years, which this woman had ignited without even trying.

Why not play with it, and her—see how far she wished to take it? It wasn't as if he would be risking anything. At thirty-one, he was even more cynical and ruthless than he had been five years ago. No way would she be able to get under his skin and fray the tight leash he kept around his emotions, the way that virginal girl had once done.

And who said she even wanted to? She was a journalist. She had to know how to use an attraction like this to her advantage—despite the pretence of nerves. The tremor in her voice, the wary tension in her gaze and the white knuckles were probably a carefully rehearsed act. But, even so, it was a good act. And an original approach, which he found surprisingly beguiling. After all, when was the last time he'd been treated to the thrill of the chase?

'Fire away, Lacey' he said, husky desire deepening his voice as he said her name again, his gaze still locked on hers, daring her to look away.

She blinked, the flicker of panic unmistakeable, but then she took a deep breath and let it out again. The movement made her breasts lift against her blouse.

Lust gathered like a fireball in his groin. He crossed his arms and leant his butt against the desk, gratified when her gaze lingered for a second on the bulge of his biceps in the fitted shirt.

Bingo.

Her gaze rose, but alongside the turmoil he could now see a fierce determination not to be intimidated.

A slow smile spread across his lips.

Good luck with that, Lacey.

'Mr Cade, I'm sorry to disturb you, but the helicopter is ready to depart now for Paris.'

Oh, thank You, God.

The knots in Lacey's gut loosened as Brandon Cade's executive assistant interrupted them signalling the end of the longest twenty minutes of her life.

What had made her think seeing this man again would be doable? Every single thing about him still disturbed her. The intense focus in his dark, penetrating green gaze. The way his body had filled out in the last five years—his biceps bulging under the starched cotton of his tailored shirt every time he crossed his arms over his broad chest, his suit trousers stretching over his thighs as he leaned on the desk in front of her. The gruff murmur of his voice which prickled over her skin every time he spoke. The way he said her name with a deliberate intimacy, which was clearly meant to disarm any woman who came within a ten-mile radius. Sitting less than two feet from him, no wonder her pheromones were toast.

Everything about him was imposing, exciting, overwhelming, just as it had been five years ago. But then she'd been an untried girl. Now she was a mother, a career woman, a proper journalist—even though, from the hooded look in his eyes, she knew he didn't rate her as one.

How did he still have the power to unsettle her so completely? Maybe because he wasn't just physically imposing any more, though the chemistry between them was still disturbingly volatile. Now so many things about him reminded her of her little girl.

Their little girl.

Given the brevity of the encounter which had created Ruby, it had been easy to persuade herself Cade had contributed virtually nothing to her daughter's DNA, but seeing him up close and personal, in broad daylight for a full twenty minutes... Not so much.

Ruby had the same mossy-green eyes with hints of steel. When Lacey had first forced herself to look at him properly, she'd recognised the colour with startling clarity. But, whereas the colour of Ruby's irises was sweet and beguiling, and so innocent, on Brandon Cade it was completely the opposite. The look in his eyes was so harsh, and yet so sharply observant, she'd been struggling to breathe, scared he could read all her secrets.

Ruby also had the same dimple in her left cheek. But, whereas on Ruby that dimple looked endearing, appearing whenever she giggled, on Brandon Cade it signalled cynical amusement, not innocent joy... Unlike Ruby's, his smiles weren't cute, they were smug and predatory. When Brandon Cade's sensual lips curved and the playful dent in his cheek appeared, Lacey's heartbeat accelerated and her breathing clogged in her lungs, making her feel like a mouse being played with by a panther.

But what was far worse than that smug, cynical smile was the way it could beckon the thoughtless, foolish girl out of hiding again. The girl who had become completely enthralled by the endorphin rush of his attention, enough to do stupid things.

Except you don't regret that stupid thing, because it gave you Ruby.

'I guess that's my cue to leave, then. Thank you for your time, Mr Cade.' She swallowed down the lump of guilt, trying to keep her expression bland as she clicked off her phone and shoved it into her bag. 'I'll email over a copy of the piece for your final approval,' she began to babble, the relief making her light-headed. 'But, until then, I'll get out of your hair.'

The truth was she'd managed to prise absolutely nothing of any use for a decent profile piece. Cade had batted away any of the remotely probing questions she'd had the guts to ask with practised ease. But she really didn't care. For once, she wasn't going to stress about her by-line. She would wax lyrical about his imposing presence, his stunning good looks and the effect of being trapped in a room with him for twenty agonising minutes…with every one of her senses on high alert…and get the art department to source some photos of him looking devastating in a tuxedo to illustrate the piece and leave it at that.

Melody would be furious Lacey hadn't managed to get any exclusive titbits out of him, anything remotely personal, but had her editor really expected her to? Honestly, the real purpose of a piece like this was to make the readership jealous of her as a journalist getting to meet the man, and overawed by how glamourous the magazine was to get this kind of access, and she'd achieved that much.

If they only knew just how close she'd got to him. Once.

She stood, ignoring the wobble in her knees, the memory which she'd had locked in her solar plexus threatening to erupt again. But as she prepared to shoot out of the room, his voice—low and deep—stopped her in her tracks.

'Not so fast, Lacey.'

She swung back to find him watching her with the challenging glint in his eyes she'd noticed several times already. As if he were enjoying her discomfort, like the panther he was.

'Why don't you accompany me?' he said, his tone casual, that all-seeing gaze anything but.

'After all, you've hardly had a chance to ask me anything interesting.'

'Accompany you where?' she stuttered, confused now, as well as wary and impossibly turned on. His searing gaze swept over her before returning to her face. Could he see her pulse hammering her throat like a heavyweight champ? Or her nipples hardening painfully under her blouse?

His lips quirked in that almost-smile again, not just smug and cynical now, but challenging, provocative and loaded with innuendo.

She took an uneven breath, trying to ease the vice clamped around her ribcage.

Breathe, Lacey, breathe. You've got this.

'To Paris, of course,' he said, the loaded smile widening.

The devastating dimple appeared as if by magic—making him look like his daughter... And yet *so* not. The vice cinched tight.

'You're not serious?' she managed.

Why was he toying with her? And why was he looking at her like that? As if her answer mattered to him, when she knew it couldn't.

'Actually, I'm deadly serious,' he said, the smile sharpening, his gaze narrowing. 'As it happens, I need a plus one for the Durand Ball tonight.'

'But I'm a celebrity journalist,' she blurted out.

She'd sensed his hostility towards her profession as soon as she walked into his office. Weirdly, that had been easier to handle than the strange atmosphere which had built between them during the course of the interview… Watchful and wary at first, but eventually becoming provocative, charged with possibilities, none of which Lacey knew she should entertain.

At first she was sure she had imagined the abrupt change in his attitude—from hostile to fascinated. She had dismissed it as a throwback to that delusional girl who had been spellbound by his interest five years ago—until their chemistry had detonated and derailed her life.

But she could feel it in the air again now, rioting over her skin, awakening her already far too responsive body, pulsing at her core—and making her yearn to say yes to his proposal, even though she knew she shouldn't.

She couldn't fall under his spell again. Because, not only would she be the only one who would get burned, but this time it wouldn't just be her in the firing line. It would be her daughter. The little girl she'd kept a secret from this man for five years— for good reason.

One dark eyebrow arched, the smile twisting his lips, not just devastating now but also disturbingly intuitive. 'Precisely—isn't this just the sort of opportunity you want? To see me in my natural habitat?'

It was a fair question. And one she had no idea how to answer without revealing more than she should. He hadn't recognised her, and she had to be pathetically grateful for that. But he was a sharply intelligent and extremely cynical and intuitive man, and she really didn't want to give him any reason to be suspicious.

'Yes, but…do you really want to give me that kind of access?' she asked. They both knew she wouldn't be able to put anything into the article he didn't approve of, but giving a journalist access to his social life was unprecedented. 'Especially after what happened with Misty,' she added.

To her dismay, though, instead of looking offended or annoyed by the intrusive comment, he simply stared at her for a moment. Then the dimple in his cheek jumped and he let out a deep, rusty chuckle.

'Touché,' he murmured, then levelled that searing gaze on her again, setting off another series of bonfires. The twinkle in his green eyes was disturbingly captivating, though, because for the first time he looked genuinely amused. 'Are you planning to write a tell-all article about my sexual prowess, then, Lacey?'

Flaming colour exploded in her cheeks at the deliberately provocative statement. 'No, of course not! I'm a journalist, I'm not interested in your sexual prowess…' she protested, a bit too much.

He was still laughing at her. She could see it in his eyes and the twitching dimple.

'So there shouldn't be a problem, then, should there?' he said, as if it were a question when clearly it wasn't.

'I suppose not,' she said.

She only realised the concession she'd inadvertently made when he added, 'I assume you have your passport with you, to get past the security on your way in?'

'Yes, but…' she began, but before she could say more he glanced past her.

'Have Jennifer book a suite at the George V for Ms Carstairs tonight, Daryl,' he said.

Lacey's cheeks ignited all over again at the realisation Daryl had just witnessed their whole compromising conversation. But she didn't really have time to contemplate the true horror of that indignity before Cade spoke again.

'And tell the pilot she'll be accompanying us.'

'But wait,' she said as he cupped her elbow to lead her out of his office.

She stumbled to a stop. The brush of his fingers was electric—just as it had been five years ago.

He frowned as she tugged her arm free. Had he felt it too? He must have.

'I don't have anything to wear to a ball,' she managed, clinging to the practical as she instinctively rubbed her elbow where his fingers had touched.

And I have a four-year-old daughter who I'm supposed to be reading a bedtime story tonight.

He nodded, still watching her, the amusement gone from his eyes. He *had* felt it… Why did that make the conflagration at her core so much worse? The guilt started to engulf her… Not just because she would have to leave the precious bedtime ritual she and Ruby enjoyed so much to her sister Milly tonight but because she had to deny her daughter's existence to the man in front of her. The man who was also responsible for Ruby, even though he didn't know it.

You made that decision five years ago with no regrets. Ruby's yours, not his. You chose to have her. You chose not to involve him.

He'd cut her out of his life that night, quickly and ruthlessly, wrenching her out of the cloud of afterglow and thrusting her into cold, hard reality as she'd lain on that desk, her heart hammering and her breasts still tender from his kisses.

'That should not have happened, and it won't happen again. The condom appears to have split, so if there are any consequences contact my office and I will deal with it.'

She tried to remember the cruelty of his dismissal that night, but the guilt and shame pressed against her throat as other even more disturbing sensations flooded her system. Sensations which had derailed her common sense once before.

His gaze lifted from her burning face back to his assistant. 'Have Jennifer arrange for a stylist to come to the hotel and dress Ms Carstairs.'

'Yes, Mr Cade.'

Cade lifted his arm as his assistant shot out of the room to do his bidding, but she noticed he was careful not to touch her again. Perhaps she had a mite more power here than she realised.

'After you, Lacey,' he said.

But I haven't agreed to go.

She should tell him where to stick his arrogant assumptions. But as she looked into his eyes, the deep jade so much like her daughter's, it occurred to her this might be the only chance she'd ever get to really get to know this man. Or at least, to get to know him enough to find out if she'd made the right decision five years ago never to tell him about his child.

Perhaps it was time she stopped running from that reckless girl and found out if Ruby's father deserved to know he had the sweetest, smartest, most engaging child in the known universe.

CHAPTER THREE

.

'INCREDIBLE WORK, LACEY, you just got yourself a promotion. You're now our star writer. But how on earth did you manage to get Cade to invite you to Paris?'

I have no idea.

Lacey stood on the ornate balcony of the luxury Parisian hotel suite, gazing at the Eiffel Tower glittering in the distance, as she gripped her phone and struggled to come up with a coherent answer for her editor.

'Um, I think maybe he wants to set the record straight. About Misty,' she managed, although she didn't believe that for a second.

The truth was she had no clue what Cade's motives were any more. It had been four hours since he'd left her at the door to the suite, and she hadn't seen him since.

She'd tried to engage him in conversation during the helicopter ride to Paris, to keep up the pretence she was still on assignment. But with the noise in the chopper it had been impossible, and anyway, Cade had seemed keen to ignore her as soon as they'd strapped in.

Thank God.

After the intensity of the twenty minutes in his office, she'd been relieved at his taciturn behaviour. She'd needed time to gather her wits—not to mention fire off a quick text to her sister Milly, asking her to put Ruby to bed tonight and drop her off at her nursery tomorrow.

As usual, her younger sister—who had lived with her since before Ruby had been born—had been happy to step up. Milly had been more like a second mum than an aunt to Lacey's daughter and Ruby adored Milly right back. Lacey knew her daughter wouldn't question Mummy needing to work late too much…

But that hadn't stopped the guilt from strangling her once she'd found herself in the lavish three-room suite at the mercy of a scarily efficient French stylist, being fitted for a stunning jewelled evening gown and styled to within an inch of her life by a team of hairdressers and make-up artists.

What am I actually doing here? I couldn't feel more out of my depth if I were trying to land a space shuttle on Mars.

'By inviting a *Splendour* journalist to the Durand Ball?' Melody laughed. 'It's too delicious. We can totally play up the Cinderella angle. The readers will love it. A hard-working single mum who gets to go to the ball on the arm of—'

'Absolutely not, Melody.' Fear wrapped around

Lacey's torso as she cut into her editor's excited pitch. 'I don't want Ruby mentioned in the piece. My daughter's not for public consumption.' And she sure as heck didn't want Brandon Cade reading about Ruby when he reviewed the piece. She'd kept her secret safe from Cade for this long. She certainly didn't want it revealed on a technicality before she was ready.

'But it's such a great angle.' Melody sighed, and Lacey could almost hear her editor pouting from two hundred miles away.

'Please, Melody, let me handle the story. He seems surprisingly cooperative. I can give you a great piece out of this, all the glitz and glamour of the Durand Ball and a night as Brandon Cade's date. We really don't need Ruby to go for the Cinderella angle,' she added, trying not to cringe so hard Melody could hear it.

She was hardly Cinderella. She had a good career, which she'd worked her socks off to create from the bonfire of being kicked to the kerb by Cade Inc five years ago. She had even earned enough to afford a mortgage on a small two-bedroom flat in Hackney last year. But she guessed it wouldn't be too much of a stretch to pitch herself as the starry-eyed, cash-strapped social outcast if Melody insisted on a Cinderella angle.

She didn't have any spare income once all the bills and Ruby's childcare were paid for. And she hadn't had a social life since Ruby had been born, keen to spend every waking minute she wasn't working with her little girl. And, even though she reported on the uber-rich and famous, she had no first-hand experience of the exclusive billionaire lifestyle Brandon Cade took for granted.

Except once, five years ago, when she'd ended up with a last-minute invite to the launch of Cade Inc's new cable channel at a Soho nightclub and had entered his rarefied world for one life-changing night.

She glanced at the sparkling jewelled fabric of the evening gown which draped luxuriously over her figure, making her slender curves look a lot less boyish than usual. The lingerie Madame Laurent had insisted she wear under the gown even made her breasts look like more than an A-cup.

She could feel the jewelled pins in her hair tugging at her scalp to anchor the hair extensions the hairstylist had spent hours arranging into a gravity-defying chignon. And imagined the smoky eyeliner, the glittery eyeshadow, the sculpted foundation and the glossy lipstick which had made her unrecognisable when the make-up artist had finally allowed her to look in the mirror.

She already felt so far outside her comfort zone, she was practically on the Moon, and that was before she factored in Cade's effect on her pulse rate.

She needed to get that reaction under control ASAP, before Cade finally showed up to escort her downstairs.

'Fine,' Melody said flatly, going all business again. 'I guess you're in charge after getting this incredible opportunity for us. But, if you can weasel any details about his feelings on the Misty Good-night situation when his guard's down, all the better.'

But his guard is never down. And, anyway, he'll nix anything he doesn't like.

She bit off the thought. 'Of course.'

She heard the sharp rap on the suite's exterior door, her heartbeat pummelling her throat with an-other one-two punch as she ended the call.

She jammed the phone into the exquisite clutch bag, also supplied by Madame Laurent.

Her thundering heartbeat began to deafen her as she walked through the dark, empty suite, her jew-elled heels sinking into the thick silk carpeting, the lights from the city behind her reflecting off the pol-ished antique furniture.

And gulped down the rising panic.

This is a golden opportunity to get to know Ru-by's father, and forgive that foolish girl from a life-time ago. End of.

'He can't intimidate you unless you let him,' she whispered to herself, then swung the door open with a bravado she didn't feel.

And almost choked. *Wow!*

Brandon Cade stood with his back to her—his broad shoulders blocking out the muted light from the hallway—in a black tuxedo perfectly tailored to spotlight his muscular torso, narrow hips and long legs. The dark hair, shaved close to his scalp, only accentuated the perfect shape of his skull.

He turned, and those moss-green eyes locked on her face, making her breath squeeze in her lungs. His gaze skimmed down—insolent, possessive—to take in the sleek, shimmering gown which suddenly felt completely transparent.

Her breathing stopped altogether, making her lightheaded, and suddenly she was that artless, innocent girl again, trapped in the laser beam of Brandon Cade's attention, yearning for his approval, her heart thundering so hard against her ribcage she was surprised it didn't leap out of her chest.

His eyes narrowed as his gaze lifted to her chignon.

'What happened to your hair?' he asked. 'It looks as if it's grown several feet in a few hours.'

The offhand comment released the breath she'd been holding. She forced herself to drag in another.

'It's magic,' she said. 'Courtesy of Gigi, my new hairstylist. And several feet of someone else's hair.'

He let out a gruff chuckle, then offered her his elbow. 'I guess we better get to the ball, then, before they ask for it back.'

She placed her fingertips on his forearm, her breathing accelerating all over again as a muscle tensed under the suit fabric and she captured his scent—clean soap and spicy cologne, an aroma she remembered far too vividly from five years ago.

He tugged her towards him until she could feel the hard line of his body against hers, then led her to the hotel lift as her heart attempted to punch its way out of her chest again.

Fabulous.

How had she ended up at the mercy of this hard,

indomitable man a second time? And how on earth was she going to keep her secrets—and her unruly senses—safe from him for an entire night?

Cinderella, hold my beer.

'Your date tonight is *très belle*, Cade, but also a surprise,' Maxim Durand, the billionaire vintner hosting tonight's ball to celebrate the spring bud-burst in his vineyards, murmured in Brandon's ear.

Brandon let out a harsh laugh as he stared at Lacey, who had been chatting with Durand's British wife Cara and his four-year-old son Pascal ever since they had arrived.

Durand was so damn proud of his family, it seemed he couldn't resist showing them off at every available opportunity. Brandon had to admit the guy's kids were pretty cute, although the way the toddler in Maxim's arms had been staring at him all night was starting to unnerve him.

He knew nothing about kids, except what he could remember about being a child himself—not a feeling he wanted to revisit.

'Why a surprise?' he asked absently, although he knew why—more than a few people had commented on his decision to invite a feature writer from a celebrity magazine tonight. This was the sort of exclusive event where the press stayed outside. But, then again, Lacey didn't seem to be taking advantage of the opportunity he'd given her… Which only made him more uneasy. Why hadn't she?

He'd heard her staggered gasp as he had guided

her into the palatial ballroom. Once attached to the private opera house next door, the hotel's historic event space had been built during the reign of Napoleon III, when pomp and circumstance had been a way of life in Paris. Gold chandeliers hung from a ceiling decorated in artwork depicting a host of Greek deities. Marble columns, sculpted statues—of yet more naked Greeks!—and bronze busts adorned the ballroom's hidden alcoves and added to the gilded splendour.

The sound of a chamber orchestra echoed off polished marble but was drowned out by the chatter of conversation and the clink of glass wear and fine china from the lavish buffet of *cordon bleu* cuisine laid out in the adjacent banqueting hall. Once the reception was over, there would be a performance from Paris's premiere ballet and then dancing of a very different kind to an A-list band who usually filled stadiums.

Everyone who was anyone in business, politics and entertainment was here tonight, presenting a smorgasbord of the kind of celebrities who guarded their privacy almost as fiercely as he did.

He'd been waiting for Lacey to sneak off, so he would have an excuse to think the worst of her, but she'd seemed subdued and tense, unwilling or unable to make the most of this golden career opportunity.

'Don't I always date beautiful women?' he added. But, even as he said the words, he couldn't help being far too aware of the unfamiliar hitch in his heartbeat which he'd been struggling to control ever since he'd turned in the hallway upstairs to see his date in that damn evening gown.

The sight was still playing havoc with his control even now. Lacey Carstairs wasn't just beautiful, she was stunning—but in a wholly unconventional way. Those cat-like eyes had seemed even more sultry and alluring thanks to the glittery gunk on her lids. The shimmering fabric of the gown skimmed over her curves like a second skin, accentuating her colt-ish beauty and highlighting her pert breasts. When he added in the glossy sheen on her lips, which had made the desire to kiss her all but unbearable, was it any surprise he couldn't take his eyes off her? He even found himself mesmerised by that elaborate hairdo, his fingers itching to pluck out the pins and sink his fingers into the short cap of curls hiding beneath.

The need to touch, taste and torment every inch of her until she begged had been driving him nuts all evening, even though he'd begun to question the decision to invite her tonight as soon as they'd boarded the helicopter in London.

'Yes, but you don't usually date celebrity journalists, *mon ami*,' Durand clarified, the wry amusement in his tone suggesting he wasn't so much irritated by Cade's choice of guest, more intrigued. 'I thought you had learned your lesson with the last one.'

Misty hadn't been a reporter, she'd been a self-publicist on social media, but he got Durand's point. He wasn't an impulsive guy, so where the hell had the decision to bring Lacey to this event even come from? And why had he only been more determined to get her here when she'd tried to put him off?

Had he fallen for the oldest trick in the book— a woman playing hard to get? And why couldn't he shake the feeling her reticence, her nerves, were one hundred percent genuine—and had nothing to do with the event and everything to do with him? He was used to women finding him intimidating, but he'd never been so aware of their feelings before now, so attuned to every tiny indrawn breath, every tensed muscle.

His awareness of her had only made him more determined to find out every damn thing he could as soon as he'd escorted her to her suite. So he'd spent an hour earlier checking her out on the Internet. Only to discover precisely nothing. How come a celebrity journalist didn't have any kind of Internet footprint—not one single social media account? Almost as if she'd appeared from nowhere two years ago when she'd got her first by-line at *Splendour*.

And how come her mysterious past hadn't done a damn thing to stem his desire? He didn't like secrets or surprises. And recklessness wasn't one of his go-to emotions either. But the desire to take her to bed was becoming more intense, the more unsettled he became, rather than less so.

Not good.

'Although, I must say, Cara seems to like her very much, and she happens to be an excellent judge of character,' Durand added, the pride in his voice unmistakeable for his pretty blonde wife—whose staggeringly large baby bump made Brandon wonder if Durand kept the poor woman permanently pregnant. 'Also, your date has been here over an hour and no one has complained yet about her.'

'I guess she's on her best behaviour,' Brandon mused, not sure it mattered to him any more.

His reaction to Lacey Carstairs had been swifter and a lot more intense than usual. But surely all he needed to do was satisfy it? He certainly wasn't remotely scared of a sexual attraction which would be easily handled once they both indulged it. Her contrary behaviour, the nerves, the guilelessness, the secrecy, and that strange something which kept tugging at his subconscious, had intrigued him, that was all.

'This woman may be more of a keeper than you are used to,' the vintner said pensively as his young daughter tugged his hair—finally getting bored with unnerving Brandon.

'*A keeper?* Yeah, right.' Brandon's laugh released the tension in his gut. He didn't do permanent, not with women—not really with anyone—because he never let anyone get that close. 'I don't think so, pal. But what makes you say that?'

Lacey wasn't a keeper, not for him anyway. But he'd always respected Durand's opinion. The man had come from nothing and built a global empire, and he was surprisingly astute.

'Because my son likes her very much too. Your Ms Carstairs is a natural with children, warm and affectionate and honest—not qualities I have noted previously in British tabloid journalists.'

Brandon frowned, Durand's observation only increasing his confusion.

Warmth? Affection? Honesty?

Since when had he prized those qualities in a date? Precisely never. Shouldn't her abilities as a child whisperer make her exceedingly dull, instead of intoxicating?

Durand seemed amused by his confusion, but was forced to make his excuses as his daughter's giggles turned to tired tears.

'It is time we put our children to bed,' he said with remarkable patience as the little girl began to tug his hair again.

The three of them made their way across the ballroom. But, as Brandon approached, Lacey's eyes locked on him—and for one arresting moment she looked like a doe trapped in a hunter's rifle sites.

Heat pumped into his groin on cue.

Durand greeted his wife, pressing his hand to the small of her back and leaning down to kiss her cheek. Cara smiled at her husband and daughter, her eyes full of an unguarded affection Brandon found disconcerting. But then he noticed Lacey staring at the couple too, and an undisguised longing flashed across her face.

Something uncomfortable and wholly unfamiliar streaked through Brandon.

What was that about?

You're not actually jealous, are you?

He forced himself to relax as the Durands excused themselves to take their children to bed. As the cou-

ple left, Lacey's gaze was still fixed on Durand and
his wife and children.

'What a wonderful family,' Lacey murmured, the
wistful comment not helping untie the knot in Brandon's gut. 'They seem so happy together.'

He glanced after the Durands. 'I guess.'

She seemed lost in thought for a moment, but then
she turned to him, the look in her eyes curious and
strangely sad. 'You don't think so?'

Her tone was casual, and the question seemed innocuous, but her gaze was focussed on him as if his
answer was important to her.

He'd been expecting her to attempt to pry details
about his personal life out of him for her article. His
opinion of the Durands' marriage hadn't been on his
radar of questions to deflect, so he shrugged and
gave her an honest answer.

'Maxim and Cara probably think they're happy
now, but I doubt it will last.'

The curious expression died, but something leapt
into her eyes that looked oddly like pity. *What the
hell?*

'Why would you think that? When it's obvious
they're devoted to each other?' Lacey asked, not
quite able to hide her horror at Brandon Cade's cynical observation. Or the wave of sympathy engulf-
ing her.

She knew she shouldn't be shocked and she certainly shouldn't feel sorry for him. The man was
a powerful billionaire, not some lost boy. But, re-

gardless, her skin chilled despite the warmth of the ballroom.

He shrugged, the movement deceptively casual. 'You didn't know Maxim before he met Cara,' he said. 'I did. No one could have been further from the family-man type. Except me.'

'You don't think a person can change?'

His gaze became flat and suspicious.

He probably thought she was asking about his views on the Durands' marriage to add to her piece. Nothing could be further from the truth—she might write celebrity features, but she had her principles.

She had promised Cara Durand any conversation they had would be off the record, but her job provided the cover she needed to probe Brandon's views on love and marriage.

He laughed, cynicism highlighting the gold shards in his irises. The dimple reappeared in his cheek, but his smile reminded her less and less of her baby girl. How could one man be so cynical, he would even doubt the sincerity of the Durands' affection for each other?

'Not really,' he said. 'Because whatever happened in Maxim's past to make him so ruthless can never be changed.'

What happened to you, Brandon, to make you so ruthless and cynical too?

The question echoed in her head. She had to bite her lip to stop herself from asking it. But it didn't stop the sympathy from pulsing in her chest.

'And why would he want to change it?' he added,

his gaze searching her face, the heat as disturbing as the confidence in his own cynicism. 'When those parts of his past have to be the reason he had the drive and ambition to build so much from absolutely nothing?'

'But it's obvious Maxim Durand loves his wife *and* his children more than anything else,' she said. 'Which suggests he would happily give up all his success rather than risk losing them,' she finished, knowing she wasn't talking about Maxim Durand any more.

People's priorities changed when they had children. She could never have imagined loving anyone as much as she loved Ruby—from the minute she'd been born. She would always put Ruby's needs first now, above everything. But it made her unbearably sad to realise Ruby's father might well not have the capacity to do the same.

The truth was, as a nineteen-year-old, alone and pregnant, she hadn't told him of his child's existence because she'd been scared—not just of his power and what he might do, but also because of her own weakness. If he'd demanded she have an abortion, would she have been strong enough to insist on making her own choice?

Weirdly, though, his predictable responses to her questions weren't helping her with the guilt one bit. Because now she felt sad for him *and* Ruby. What if he *could* change, as Maxim Durand had done, but she had denied him the opportunity to find out?

'Spoken like a true romantic,' he said, the obvious distain in his tone cutting deep. She wasn't a romantic, she was a realist, because she'd had to be.

'I never figured you people actually believed all the sentimental hogwash you publish about guys like me,' he added.

He was laughing at her now, the harsh glint in his eyes as arrogant as it was cynical. The desire to wipe that smirk off his too-handsome face was irresistible.

'Sentimental hogwash, huh? I had no idea you were such an avid reader of *Splendour* magazine,' she managed, the tart reply going someway to cover the sympathy for him still pulsing in her chest.

He chuckled. 'Not so much, but I've got to say, you've made me wonder if I've been missing out.' His gaze intensified, but this time she didn't just see heat, she saw approval. 'You're not at all what I expected.'

The surprise that she'd impressed him was swiftly followed by concern as the green fire in his eyes made her thigh muscles loosen and the hot spot in her belly throb.

'And, while I don't do clichés as a rule, I've got to admit you're even hotter when you fight back, Lacey.'

His gaze locked on hers, the heat and purpose in it sizzling over her skin and making her nipples squeeze into aching peaks. But his approval was so much more intoxicating…and terrifying.

'Hot enough to make me break my golden rule,' he continued.

'Which is?' she asked, trying for indifference, but getting breathlessness instead.

'Never to sleep with a woman who thinks she can change me.'

He cupped her cheek. She jolted, the rough texture of his thumb trailing over her lips, and the fiercely possessive light in his eyes, making it impossible for her to look away. Or get her lungs to function.

The lights from the chandeliers dimmed as the guests were directed into the adjoining salon to enjoy the special performance of the Paris Opera Ballet. But the two of them remained in the ballroom, co-cooned in the darkness, suddenly alone in the cavernous space but for the staff. Lacey's breathing accelerated, all the reasons why she shouldn't let him touch her queuing up in her head, but her body refused to listen as his fingers curved around her neck and drew her towards him.

'You really are exquisite,' he said, his mouth lowering to hers, his scent filling her senses, her heart beating double time.

Why had she never felt like this with any other man? Was it just that Brandon Cade was the father of her child, the only man she had ever made love to? Or was it even more specific than that?

She placed trembling palms on his waist, her hands reaching inside his tuxedo jacket. His stomach muscles tensed.

'Madame Laurent and Gigi will be pleased you think so,' she said.

He laughed, the husky sound strained, the rich

approval in his gaze as heady now as it had been once before.

'I'm not talking about the gown.' His gaze flicked to her chignon. 'Or the hair.' Warm hands caught her waist and drew her close until she could feel exactly how much he desired her. 'It's what's underneath I want.'

She blinked, the arousal flowing through her body on a tidal wave of desperation. Now, as then, she couldn't seem to make her brain function because all she could feel was the need.

'That sounds like a very bad idea,' she whispered, trying to make herself mean it.

Fierce heat flared in his gaze, and suddenly his hands had moved to grasp her cheeks, to lift her face to his.

'I know,' he murmured against her lips, his voice hoarse as the heat pulsed and throbbed at her core. But then his lips captured hers in a forceful, demanding kiss. She gasped, shocked by the brutal yearning which surged from her core. His tongue delved into the recesses of her mouth, controlling her, possessing her, wanting her, needing her with a ferocity she remembered.

The part of her brain still clinging to sanity knew she should tell him to stop, but the heady joy of being wanted again—by him—was far too raw and all-consuming to allow her to do anything but surrender to the moment.

A moment she hadn't even realised she had been waiting to relive for five years.

She found herself kissing him back with the same fervour—no longer the young girl happy to absorb all the sensations battering her. Now she was a woman, with needs of her own. Her tongue tangled with his, her hands fisted in his starched shirt as she tugged him closer. Her body vibrated with yearning as she reached up on tiptoes and met his hunger with all the need and longing from so long ago.

The kiss became carnal, and devastating, a battle for supremacy. She ripped her mouth from his—trying to regain her sense of self, her equilibrium—but it remained out of reach, the harsh rasps of her breathing making her lightheaded.

His expression became fierce and determined as his hands skimmed down the gossamer silk of her gown, shattering her senses all over again. His hands landed on her bottom to press her into the thick ridge in his trousers and his mouth found the hammering pulse point in her neck.

She gasped, shuddered, as she lost herself again in his devastating caresses.

Her head fell back, her own fingers tensing and releasing, her mind drifting into the forbidden zone where nothing mattered except feeding this incessant hunger.

Suddenly he wrenched himself away.

His gaze focussed on her face, and his palms rose to cup her cheeks. Satisfaction roared through her as she noticed his hands trembled.

Yes, she wanted him, but he wanted her right back. She hadn't imagined that five years ago. All this time she had blamed that girl for allowing herself to be used, for not reading the signs. But she wasn't that needy girl any more who would be devastated when this night was over. She knew the score.

He swore softly, then growled. 'I want to take you to bed.'

She knew she should say no. But why did this have to be about Ruby? Why couldn't it just be about them? He didn't know who she was, didn't know he had once destroyed her.

She'd been careful, patient and pragmatic for so long, solely focussed on building a new life, a better life, for her and her little girl. But during the last five years she'd also hated the untried girl she had been that night, for giving herself to him so easily, for falling halfway in love with him after a few hours without ever really knowing him, and for allowing herself to be destroyed by his rejection.

Didn't that girl deserve the chance to enjoy this chemistry again, but on her terms now instead of his?

She let the heady excitement course through her veins. And nodded.

CHAPTER FOUR

THE NEXT FEW MINUTES—as Brandon Cade dragged her out of the ballroom, through the heritage hotel's ornate lobby area and up the grand staircase to their suites—went by in a blur.

Lacey felt as if she were floating on a wave of euphoria…and dread.

The voice inside her head, demanding she stop this madness, was drowned out by the deafening thuds of her heartbeats and the brutal yearning burning like a hot brick at her core.

'Your suite or mine?' Brandon demanded, his voice raw, when they reached the first-floor hallway.

'I… I don't know,' she managed, her throat drying to parchment.

'Mine's bigger,' he supplied.

Seconds later, her mind still reeling, her body still yearning, still pliant, she found herself standing in the shadowy splendour of the hotel's Presidential Suite. He led her past upholstered sofas, ornate furniture, a spray of flowers in a priceless antique vase and out onto a large terrace, the full moon and the twinkling lights of the Eiffel Tower so close, it seemed as if she could reach out and touch them.

But then he swung her round. And all she could see was him. Tall, handsome, indomitable. He tugged off his jacket, dumped it on the marble tiles then grasped her hips in urgent hands and pulled her into his body.

His mouth fastened back on her neck, finding the pulse point, exploiting it ruthlessly and without mercy. She grasped his head, the short bristles of hair sending yet more sensation shimmering south as she held him to her, let him feast. Blood rushed to her breasts, trapped against his hard chest.

He lurched back. The harsh rasps of their breathing tore through the quiet night. He laughed, the sound husky, strained, and she wondered how she had amused him. But then he clasped her chin and lifted her face to his.

'Promise me this won't end up in your article.'

She blinked, the request disorientating and confusing at first—the intoxicating hunger rushing through her body so turbo-charged, she couldn't think.

But then it all came crashing back—who she was, why she was here, what she had worked so hard to achieve... She was a grown woman with a career, a life and a little girl who could be compromised, threatened, even destroyed by this man.

You fool. The power you feel is an illusion, a trap. He holds all the power here. He always has.

She staggered back, wrenching herself out of his

embrace. She pressed a panicked hand to her head to discover the carefully styled chignon had been torn loose. The hair extension came away in her fingers—somehow a symbol of the shattered illusion.

Her breath heaved, and her heart pumped so fast, she was terrified he could hear it too.

'I... I have to leave,' she whispered.

But as she went to walk past him—to *run* past him—he snagged her wrist. 'Where are you going?'

'I can't... I can't do this. It...it would be totally unprofessional,' she said, clinging to any excuse, any way to get away from the yearning she'd foolishly unleashed downstairs—which was still charging through her body and telling her to take the risk. To indulge the pleasure without regrets.

'Are you joking?' he said. He didn't sound annoyed, just surprised.

'No, I'm not.' She twisted her wrist out of his grasp, rubbing the skin where his touch burned. 'And, FYI, I don't write porn.'

She rushed back through the suite's lavish living area, her body aching with unfed desire.

'Come back here!' he shouted.

This time, his hands captured her shoulders to drag her round, and the tremble of reaction reached right down to her soul.

'I didn't mean to insult you,' he said softly.

She clasped her arms around her waist. She had to get out before the madness took her again. But somehow she couldn't seem to move. She stood rooted to the spot as his hands caressed the bare skin, his thumb skimming over the pulse point in her neck he had devoured only moments before.

'Yes, you did,' she countered, knowing his intentions hardly mattered now. All that mattered was that she didn't give in to the sensations still pulsing at her core. He had never treated her with gentleness before, only demand. Why did the softness of his touch now, that strange feeling of possession—as if both their bodies understood he had a right to hold her—only make her heart pound harder?

He let out a gruff chuckle, self-deprecating and all the more disarming for it.

'Yeah, I guess I did.' He lifted his hands from her shoulders, raising his palms in the universal sign of surrender. 'But, in my defence,' he added, his voice losing the lilt of amusement. 'I'm a deeply cynical guy. And you're a reporter who can make a fortune out of exposing all my secrets.'

She missed the warm weight on her bare shoulders instantly, but worse was the lurch in her chest at the candid direction of the conversation. And the thought of how he had been manipulated, his private life exposed by another woman.

She'd assumed he was a man who couldn't be hurt, but maybe he could.

She'd kidded herself she had accepted his invitation to Paris to find out more about him. She could see now that had never been the whole truth.

She'd also been compelled by the incendiary chemistry which had derailed her life once before...

and made Ruby. But even so she was still desperately curious about him.

'Do you have a lot of secrets?' she asked, before she could stop herself.

'Are you asking as a reporter or a woman?' he replied.

It was a leading question. One she was wary of answering truthfully. But even so she said, 'As a woman.'

His lips curved in the half-smile. But this time, when the dimple appeared, it seemed genuine.

'Yeah, I've got a lot of secrets.' His thumb moved, brushing under her chin, then trailing down to trace the swell of her breast above the gown's bodice. His touch was subtle, alluring, devastating.

Her breathing accelerated, her heart pumping desire back.

'But then, doesn't everyone?' he added.

She jolted, her breath catching. Did he somehow know about Ruby? But, before the panic could take hold, he continued, 'It's what makes sex so exciting. Discovering a woman's secrets, figuring out all the ways to make her ache, make her moan, make her beg.'

Her breath gushed out on a staggered sigh, but with relief came the heady kick of desire as his devious thumb trailed down to circle the tight bud of her nipple, hardening beneath the silk.

Sex. This was all just about sex to him. Nothing more.

'Let me find out all your secrets, Lacey,' he whispered, his breath warm against her neck as his fingers found the tab under her arm and tugged it down. The sibilant hum of the zip releasing was deafening. But not as deafening as her racing pulse.

'I promise, not one of them will leave this suite,' he added, the seductive tone beckoning her back into madness. 'Just one night, that's all I ask.'

'Okay,' she said, on a gasp of pleasure.

'Good girl,' he said.

The bodice released, the jewelled straps of the gown falling from her shoulders as he brushed them aside.

The city lights glittered in his gaze as it roamed over her, making him look saturnine, fierce.

'Damn, you're beautiful,' he whispered.

His large hand covered the transparent lace of her bra, weighing her swollen breast in his palm. He bent his head to capture the stiff peak through the gossamer fabric.

She clasped his head, struggling to breathe now, struggling to stay upright, the warm, wet pressure so perfect, so right and yet not enough.

'I... Please... I want...' she stammered, holding his head, trying to drag him closer, to feel more, to feel it all.

'Yeah, I know,' he said, drawing back to scoop her off the floor with startling ease.

Her heart bounced in her chest as he strode into the next room with her cradled in his arms. The lavish bedroom had a large king-sized bed as its centrepiece. Through the patio doors, she could still see Paris's iconic tower, like a spear of light in the darkness, but all she could feel was the need streaking through her body as he placed her on her feet.

He turned her towards the glass. Her lacy push-up bra released, and suddenly his hands were on her naked breasts, caressing, stroking, plucking at the damp nipples. She bowed back against him, unable to protest as he lifted her arm and draped it around his neck, his hands sliding down her sides, making shocking sensation riot over her skin.

He worked the gown from her hips until it fell in a pool of glittery silk at her feet. His lips feasted on her neck, making her ache, making her beg, just as he had promised.

'Look at yourself, Lacey.'

Her eyelids fluttered open to see the decadent sight reflected in the glass. She stood naked—but for the swatch of transparent lace hiding the shadow of her sex. Her skin was so pale, her body somehow petite against the large, dark shape of him behind her.

His hands, captured, possessed, circling her breasts, making her buck and gasp.

'You're mine tonight, Lacey,' he said, the words strained and darkly compelling. His fingers slid down to glide under the lace covering her sex and locate the slick folds. She bucked against his hold as he circled the epicentre of her need. Teasing, tempting.

'Say it,' he demanded.

'Yes... I'm yours tonight,' she said, throwing caution away in the desperate pursuit of pleasure as his sure, steady fingers continued to stroke, to torment.

'Please, can you…?' The need clogged in her lungs as she offered her breasts to him, brazenly begging for his caresses.

'I want you to watch yourself, Lacey,' he said.

She forced her eyelids open again, saw her yearning body writhe against his hold in the glass.

His clever fingers found the very heart of her pleasure. At last.

'Come for me,' he commanded, beckoning forth the staggering orgasm on a brutal wave of release.

She cried out, bowed back, bucking against his perfect touch. And the pleasure soared through her as he stroked her through the shattering climax.

She collapsed against him at last. His touch was still firm, still there.

She grasped his wrist. 'Please, it's too much.'

He withdrew his hand, but then turned her to him, cradled her cheeks. His thumb trailed across her lips.

She could taste her own pleasure on his fingers. And something raw and erotic bumped and swelled at her core as he lifted her limp body into his arms and placed her on the bed.

She watched him strip off in the moonlight. Saw the sculpted muscles of his chest, the bold lines of his hip flexors, the dark line of hair that trailed through washboard abs and bloomed at his groin. Her gaze devoured the masculine beauty of his body, then settled on the column of erect flesh—so thick, so long—proving how much he wanted her.

She'd never seen him fully naked all those years

ago. Why did this feel so much more intimate, so much more overwhelming?

But then her gaze rose to his as he crawled onto the bed, trapping her yearning body against his as he stripped off her thong.

He kissed her with feverish desire, fervent desperation.

'We're not through yet, Lacey,' he said with an urgent desire which held threat as well as promise. His lips traced down her torso to torment her too-sensitive nipples, first one, then the other, licking, nipping, sucking, until she was moaning again.

His lips trailed lower, kissing her quivering flesh, now aching with desperation once more. He spread her legs, opening her completely.

'We've only just started,' he said, his breath feathering her exposed sex.

Then he touched the molten heart of her. She jolted and cried out, the sensation too much and yet not enough. Licking and probing, his devious mouth drew her moans forth until his lips captured the swollen nub and suckled hard. Her sex pulsed and throbbed, another orgasm barrelling towards her with staggering speed. The shocking climax was brutal in its intensity.

She collapsed onto the bed, struggling to gather her breath when his big body loomed above her. She watched him, dazed, disorientated, her body still awash in brutal pleasure as he rolled on a condom with clumsy fingers.

At last, he grasped her hips, positioned the huge

head of his erection at her sodden entrance then drove himself deep in one all-consuming thrust.

A guttural moan she didn't even recognise as her own echoed around the room. The slickness of her orgasms eased his entry. But, once he was lodged to the hilt, the stretched feeling she remembered was all but overwhelming.

She felt impaled, conquered, owned as the devastating waves began to build again, impossibly.

'Hold on to me…' He grunted.

She clasped his sweat-slicked shoulders and clung on as he began to move. Drawing out, pounding back, he forced her to new heights as the pleasure rolled back over her, even harder, faster and more furious than before.

This time, when release came, it slammed into her, sending her soaring into a delirious, welcome oblivion.

She heard him shout out from many miles away as he charged after her into the same stunning, scary, bottomless abyss.

Brandon pulled out of the woman beneath him, bracing his arms to stop from crushing her. He flopped back on the bed beside her, the last of the mind-blowing orgasm still rippling through him and turning his mind, and his senses, to mush.

What the hell was that?

His body felt altered somehow, the desire still pulsing through his system and making him feel more alive, more attuned to another human being than he ever had before…except maybe once.

He frowned and turned to see Lacey's bare shoulder. She'd rolled away from him and curled in on herself. The rise and fall of her breathing suggested she had dropped into a deep sleep.

Who is she?

Why had she responded to him with such unrestrained enthusiasm? And why had each soft moan, each sweet sob, each shudder of surrender, only made him more ravenous? More desperate to push her further, to take more?

Had it really all been an act?

But, even as he tried to convince himself, he couldn't. He was a good judge of people and he knew her reaction, when he'd insisted she keep any intimacy between them off the record, had been absolutely genuine. She'd been upset and determined to walk away.

He still wasn't entirely sure why he hadn't let her. Because, even before he'd got her naked and made her come apart in his arms—not once, not twice, but three times, with a wild abandon which had stunned him—he'd known this connection was too intense, too savage to be easily controlled.

He should wake her up, ask her to leave. He never slept with women through the night because he hated to encourage too much intimacy.

But, as he rolled towards her, his hand landing on her shoulder, he couldn't bring himself to shake her awake. Instead, his palm skimmed down the curve of her body to rest on her hip.

She stirred but remained asleep, the murmur of her breathing—and the feel of her soft skin beneath his hand—making the incessant heat gather again in his groin.

Seriously?

He sighed and inhaled her scent.

The fresh, tempting perfume she must have dabbed on her neck had faded, to be replaced by the musty scent of sex and the rich, intoxicating scent of her skin.

Rich, intoxicating... And... He shifted closer to her to gather another greedy lungful. Disturbingly familiar.

His shaft swelled against her bottom as the memories the aroma invoked slammed into him.

Another woman. A girl. So eager and responsive, she had destroyed all his caution, all his control, in the space of a few heady hours.

What the actual...? He swore and jerked away from the woman in his bed now.

How could Lacey have exactly the same smell as that girl and affect him in the same incendiary way? The girl he'd banished from his life so long ago but had never been able to fully forget.

Could she be...?

Dammit, Cade, get a grip.

He forced himself to breathe through the wave of panic and stunned arousal and waited for his exhausted mind to engage.

How could she be the same woman? Wouldn't he have recognised her immediately? And wouldn't she have said something? But then he recalled everything about her—from the minute she had entered his office that afternoon—which had provoked and aroused memories of that night five years ago.

Hell, whether she was that girl or not, was that why he had been so determined to bring her to Paris, to seduce her?

He dragged off the sheet, his skin tingling again, the coil of desire in his gut tightening from the renewed overload of sensation which Lacey seemed to trigger without even trying. Just like that girl.

How could those memories still be so vivid too?

He forced himself to get up, to get away from her. He stalked into the bathroom, closed the door then turned on one of the ambient lights. Bracing his hands on the marble vanity, he stared at his face in the mirror as the sensory overload continued to charge through his system like a wild stallion—untamed, uncontrollable.

He breathed through it, waiting for the adrenaline rush to subside. His pulse finally slowed and the strident erection subsided enough for him to think coherently.

He stripped off the condom, then washed his hands and face. The splash of cold water brought him back to his senses.

Surely Lacey couldn't be Lizzy Devlin?

But there was one easy way to find out. Because

there was another distinguishing mark on that girl he remembered far too vividly.

He walked back into the bedroom. Lacey hadn't moved, her body still curled into a foetal position, her breathing slow and even.

He switched on the bedside light, the soft glow adding a lustre to her skin, but she still didn't stir. He tugged the sheet down and watched it slide over the curve of her backside to reveal the pale flesh of her buttocks in the lamplight.

His breathing stopped and a wave of anger blind-sided him. A swear word hissed through clenched teeth.

Lacey Carstairs had a lot of explaining to do.

Starting with why the hell she hadn't mentioned he had devoured her in a similar frenzy five years ago.

But what infuriated him more was the blistering heat which followed as he examined the heart-shaped birthmark high on her right buttock—and the visceral memory of how he'd discovered it once before flowed through his system again like wildfire.

CHAPTER FIVE

LACEY JERKED AWAKE, her body still humming, her mind a mess. She blinked, aware of all the places she ached. But then it all came rushing back—the ballroom kiss, the rush of panic on the balcony of Brandon's suite, the dark deeds which had followed as she'd succumbed to his seduction. Wildly, willingly. She shivered, aware of her nakedness, and the sensations still skittering across her skin.

She shifted in the bed, the glimmer of dawn seeping into the night sky illuminating the empty space beside her. A thin strip of light glowed under the bathroom door.

Thank goodness.

Cade had to be in there, even though she couldn't hear him.

Gathering the sheet, she tucked it around herself and scooted off the bed. She needed to get back to her own room before he reappeared. She must have been asleep for hours.

She found her discarded underwear and dropped the

sheet to slip it on, wincing slightly as the lace brushed against the beard burn on her breasts, her thighs.

Classy, much?

The beautiful gown was hopelessly crushed, the creases in the jewelled silk a testament to her staggeringly ill-judged decision to revisit the catastrophic choices of her youth.

How on earth was she going to explain to Melody she'd missed most of the event? And how did she square the decision to sleep with Brandon Cade again with the knowledge she had given birth to his child and had never told him of Ruby's existence?

She tugged on the gown, scrabbling around until she found her heels.

The light from the bathroom was still on. Should she leave him a note? She dismissed the notion. Brandon Cade would be through with her now.

And, anyway, she was through with him too. So they were all good.

As long as she didn't factor in his four-year-old daughter.

Don't think about that now. Once you're back in London, you can regroup, rethink, revisit all the things you learned about him tonight.

Not that the new information she'd gathered amounted to very much. Other than the fact he still had the ability to make her lose her ever-loving mind, forget all her priorities and climax on demand.

She swallowed around the growing lump of guilt…and shame…and panic…and tiptoed out of the bedroom with her heels in her hand.

She shot through the dimly lit living area and grabbed her bag, which was sitting on a coffee table... Had she put it there? She couldn't even remember.

The staggering view of the Eiffel Tower was now lit by the red light of the approaching dawn. Gulping down an unsteady breath, she dived towards the door.

She was halfway there when a low voice—edged with fury—whispered through the darkness.

'Where are you off to, Lacey?'

She swung round, clutching her shoes and her bag, and spotted Brandon sitting in the shadows of the room, watching her.

The lump rammed her throat and her heartbeat hit warp speed.

Had he been lying in wait for her?

She cleared her throat, trying to calm her frantic pulse and speak round the rapidly expanding lump. 'I'm going back to my room.'

Then I'm getting dressed and heading for the Gare du Nord to take the first train back to London—and get the heck out of Dodge.

He turned on a light on the table beside him. He wore sweat pants and a T-shirt, his feet bare. It was the most casual clothing she'd ever seen him wear. But, when he stood up and walked towards her, it didn't make an appreciable difference to her erratic heartrate. Or the power and purpose which emanated from him.

How could he still look so overwhelming?

He cupped her cheek, making her tense, drew his

thumb across her lips—lips now red from his kisses. She let out a shuddering breath. She could still feel him inside her, taking her to places no other man had ever taken her.

Focus, Lacey, for goodness' sake.

She dragged herself away from his touch.

'Why are you in such a hurry, Lacey?' he asked as his hand dropped, but the harsh light in his eyes belied the conversational tone. 'Or should I call you Lizzy?'

She jolted. She could see the feral expression now and recognised it as anger.

Her stomach knotted, the lump of guilt and regret growing to impossible proportions.

'How long have you known?' she whispered.

And how *much* did he know?

Did he know about Ruby? About their child? The knots in her stomach became giant serpents.

But, as he continued to stare at her, her own anger surged, along with the devastating hurt she'd buried deep five years ago.

She let it burn under her breastbone now to protect herself from the shivers wracking her body, and the black hole of inadequacy threatening to open up in her chest.

So what if she'd lied to him about her identity? She refused to feel guilty about it. Refused to let him accuse her again, the way he'd once accused that foolish girl.

The girl he'd dismissed without a backward glance—and thrown away so casually.

What right did he have to be angry with her, when he had treated her so appallingly that night? And what exactly did she have to apologise for, when he had never apologised to her?

Brandon frowned, annoyed to see Lacey's initial shock turn to stubborn resistance, instead of the guilt and embarrassment he had been expecting.

That she only looked more stunning dressed in the creased gown, her short hair a mess of unruly curls, and the bold, belligerent light in her eyes turning them to a golden brown, was neither here nor there.

He wouldn't be fooled by her act a second time. Heat surged in his groin, calling him a liar.

Well, not until he'd got a few straight answers out of her—to the many, *many* questions which had been queuing up in his head while he'd been sitting in the dark for hours, waiting for her to put in an appearance. That she'd intended to run out on him, without even the courtesy of a goodbye, let alone an explanation, added to his sense of injustice.

'You may not know this, but you have a rather distinctive birthmark on your right cheek,' he said, his gaze drifting down to her bottom to make it abundantly clear exactly which cheek he was referring to. 'I noticed it the first time you tried to trick me into a commitment.'

'*Trick* you?' She sucked in a furious breath. 'I didn't try to *trick* you into anything five years ago,' she snapped, her exploding temper highlighting the gold sparks in her irises. 'You arrogant, insufferable, overbearing…' She sputtered to a stop, clearly struggling to locate an insult bad enough.

'Arrogant, insufferable, overbearing *what*, exactly, Lizzy?' he goaded, as his own fury pulsed like a ticking bomb. 'Halfwit, perhaps, given that is what you take me for?'

'Don't call me Lizzy,' she shot back. 'My name's not Lizzy any more, it's Lacey.'

'So I gather, which begs the question, why did you change it?' he sneered, letting his outrage at her deception show. 'Other than to deliberately deceive me, of course? And why did you choose not to inform me we had already met when you walked into my office this afternoon and proceeded to snare me again with your artless little act?'

'My artless little…?' Her cheeks exploded with outraged colour as her face turned a surprisingly beguiling shade of red. 'I did not *snare* you, you arrogant jerk. *You* snared *me*. *You* invited *me* to Paris, not the other way around. I tried as politely as I could to turn you down. And you refused to get the message, and refused to take no for an answer, like the overbearing halfwit you actually are.'

'Ah, yes, your not at all convincing attempt to turn down my invitation. Am I actually supposed to believe now that wasn't all part of your act too?' he sneered. 'To lure me back into your bed.'

'Oh, go to hell, I don't give a flying f—' She stopped dead, clearly making a titanic effort not to utter the swear word for no reason he could fathom.

'I don't give a flying feather duster what you do or do not believe!' she finally burst out.

He should have been even more angry, of course, but the ridiculous alternate swear word had his fury fading.

'A feather duster? *Really?*' he said, having to bite his tongue to stop from smiling.

This was not funny in the slightest. She'd tricked him, deceived him, and he still hadn't got a single straight answer out of her. But something about the way she was fighting back was making admiration for her—and her temper—build alongside the fury.

It occurred to him she was different from the girl he remembered. That girl had been quiet, subdued, deliberately close-mouthed when he'd confronted her that night about her virginity—making him sure he'd been right, that her 'sacrifice' had all been a deliberate ploy to trick him into a commitment. But this woman was a firebrand.

Her glare sharpened. 'Yes, really,' she declared. 'I try not to use profanity when I can help it,' she said with just enough strained patience to make his lips quirk again.

'Why?' he asked, because he was genuinely curious, the coy reply almost as beguiling as the rosy hue on her cheeks.

She looked away from him, but not before he caught the shadow of guilt.

What was that about? Why would she feel guilty about trying not to swear at him? It made no sense.

He tucked a knuckle under her chin. Her cheeks

had reddened even more, but she stared back at him with a boldness which only made the hunger he thought he'd tamed flare anew.

'Why are you so worried about saying the F-word?' he asked again, even curiouser now as to why she wouldn't want to answer the question. 'Are you training to be a nun?'

She didn't reply, her lips flattening into a thin line.

'Because, I have to tell you, on last night's evidence I fear you have chosen entirely the wrong vocation,' he mocked, still enjoying her temper too much.

He brushed his thumb across her lips again, unable to stop himself from touching her as she continued to glare at him defiantly. His thumb drifted down to caress the pulse fluttering in her collarbone like the wings of a trapped bird as he revelled in the awareness in her eyes, which she couldn't disguise.

'I have my reasons,' she said evasively, stepping away from his touch again. 'I need to leave.'

The fury surprised him as she turned to go, but not as much as the wrench in his chest.

'Oh, no you don't.' He grasped her wrist. 'You're not leaving until you give me a straight answer.'

What the hell was she hiding from him? And why? She wanted something from him—they all did. Eventually. So why wasn't she asking for it?

She tugged her hand free and rubbed her wrist. 'Fine, you want an answer. Here's one. You asked me why I changed my name. As if you didn't know!' She spat the words, her own temper rising.

He wasn't buying that diversionary tactic a second time, though.

'Obviously, I do not know, or I would not have asked.'

'Because you had me blacklisted,' she said, the pain that flashed across her face shocking him into silence, not least because it made the wrench in his chest throb. 'I couldn't get a job anywhere in journalism as Lizzy Devlin after that night.'

'What the hell are you talking about?' he said, genuinely perplexed, trying to remember what he'd actually said to his executive assistant the next day. He'd acted in haste, he remembered that, but he'd only asked Daryl to ensure their paths would never cross again. His kinetic, livewire response to her had rattled him. Her virginity and his complete loss of control in that damn office had rattled him even more. Not unlike his response to her tonight. But he would never have punished her in that way for something which he had eventually acknowledged was as much his fault as hers. In truth, *more* his fault than hers, given her lack of experience, whatever her intentions.

'I was summarily fired the next day,' she said, her anger now tempered by a sadness, a sense of injustice, which had the wrench in his chest widening. 'Without a reference and without any severance pay. And, when I tried to apply for other trainee jobs, I never even got a reply let alone an interview. I finally figured out why when a recruiter I applied to and who wouldn't take me on told me in confidence

I should consider changing my name. That "power-ful forces",' she continued, doing air quotes as the sheen of emotion glowed in her eyes, 'Had made Lizzy Devlin unemployable.'

He had never been one of those men who could be manipulated by a woman's tears—after all, he'd had no trouble at all withstanding Misty's big dra-matic moment when he'd informed her their affair was over. But when Lacey blinked and the sheen disappeared from her eyes, it occurred to him there was something a lot more unsettling about a woman who refused to let the tears fall.

'I wanted to be a news reporter and you took that away from me.' Her tone lost the edge of temper, loaded now with accusation and injured pride. Some-thing he could understand. After all, his father had once taken great delight in injuring his pride and making him aware he meant nothing to Alfred Cade other than being a means to an end. 'And I never un-derstood why,' she said, the anger all but gone now, to reveal the hurt beneath. 'What did I do that was so terrible that made you want to punish me? That made you think I *deserved* to be punished?'

You made me feel, too much.

He locked the thought away. Because it was lu-dicrous. She hadn't made him feel, she'd made him want her too much—that was all. So much he hadn't stopped to think, hadn't used any of his usual fi-nesse. She'd looked at him with that dewy approval in her gaze all evening, lapping up his conversa-tion, being smart, cute and disarming… And all his smooth moves with women had deserted him until they'd ended up in a grubby little office with him pounding into her as if his life had depended on it. And, when he'd discovered she was a virgin, his incendiary reaction had only shocked him more.

'Does that answer your question?' she demanded, the harsh edge returning and yanking him back to the present.

Her face was lit now by the dawn. The artful make-up of last night, the elaborate hairstyle, were gone. But somehow it didn't make her any less beautiful, and suddenly he could see that girl again—in the tilt of her eyes, the naked emotion, the forthright expression.

But, when she turned to go this time, instead of anger all he felt was regret. So when he reached for her again, his touch was gentle, his voice even more so.

'Don't…' he murmured.

She stared at him, her expression carefully remote, but still he could see the hurt.

'Don't go,' he said, before she could tug herself free. He tightened his grip on her wrist. 'I want to apologise.'

Her brows shot up. He had stunned her.

The truth was, he'd stunned himself almost as much. Even when he was in the wrong, he never apologised. Because he refused to show a weakness. But this one time, he couldn't seem to stop himself.

He'd let her take the blame for everything that had happened five years ago. Because it had been easier than examining his own behaviour, his own shocking reaction. But it was way past time he addressed that, or how was he going to handle the need now?

He still wanted her. One night had not been enough. And he intended to have her. Because he wasn't scared of his reaction any more. However volatile his response to her, it was purely physical. But, if the goal was to get her back into his bed, he needed to repair the damage he'd done. Luckily, he was an extremely goal-orientated guy.

'What for?' she said, the suspicion in her eyes crucifying him a little.

How typical of this woman not to take his unprecedented apology at face value. Was that another reason he found her so alluring—because she was proving to be a match for him in more than just the bedroom? How frustrating that he even found her contrary behaviour a turn-on.

'For what happened to your career,' he clarified. 'It was never my intention to have you blacklisted. I never even requested you be fired from Cade Inc.' Although he could see now why his ruthlessly efficient EA would have assumed as much from his remarks. No doubt Daryl had picked up on how rattled he had been by his close encounter with young Lizzy Devlin and had acted accordingly. 'I simply told my executive assistant to ensure our paths never crossed again. He clearly took that request and ran with it in a direction I had not intended.'

She stiffened slightly, and he could see he had hurt her again without meaning to. But instead of asking the obvious question…*why* had he been so determined to never to see her again?…she simply shrugged.

Great. Indifference. Just the effect he'd been aiming for.

'Right, well, thanks for clarifying that,' she said, the sarcasm not amusing him in the slightest. 'It makes me feel so much better to know my career got destroyed by accident.'

'What else do you expect me to say?' he said, becoming exasperated. 'I can't go back and change the past. That said, I will of course instruct my HR people to offer you a generous severance package for the way you were dismissed,' he finished, finally figuring out the best way to handle the situation. 'Whatever your annual salary was at the time, I'll have them double it as a one-off compensation payment.' Normally he would never admit liability but, given what had happened, and *how* it had happened, he could see she deserved restitution. And he could afford to be generous.

Last night had proved that, for whatever reason, this woman fired up his libido like no other. His sex life had been jaded for far too long. The thought of exploring this explosive chemistry in a great deal more depth excited him beyond reason. And he was more than happy to pay for the privilege.

But, instead of accepting his very generous offer, the glare reappeared. 'Is everything about money to you?'

It was his turn to flinch. 'What is the problem

now?' he asked, because he genuinely didn't get it. He'd apologised, he'd offered her compensation. What the hell else did she want?

'Let me explain it in words of one syllable,' she said, the condescending tone starting to get on his nerves. 'I. Don't. Want. Your. Money,' she added, elucidating each word as if he were an imbecile. 'I never did. *You* were the one who accused me of trying to trap you into a commitment with sex. Not once, but twice. But I never asked you for one single thing. When we slept together five years ago...'

She huffed, the colour rising up her neck to suffuse her face. 'When we slept together tonight, it happened because I've never felt that kind of need before or since. It was a moment...well, more than a moment...of madness. And I revelled in it. Believe me, I did not have any ulterior motives. For goodness' sake, all I could do when you kissed me was react. I certainly wasn't thinking, because if I had been no way would I have put myself in a position to be insulted by you a second time.' She stopped abruptly, regret tightening her features, and he knew she knew she had said far too much.

Because the heat was charging through his veins all over again and pulsing in the air between them— like lightning ready to strike.

Her eyes widened, the lurid flush highlighting her cleavage. But the arousal had dilated her pupils to black, and he could see the fierce need she felt too in the tremor of her body.

She shot round, like a doe trying to escape the

hunter, but this time he didn't hesitate. He grasped her upper arm and dragged her back. Until they were toe to toe, eye to eye, her breathing as ragged as his.

He wrapped his arms around her slender waist, notching the erection pulsing in his pants against the soft swell of her belly—and lowered his mouth to hers.

'You don't seriously think I'm going to let you leave now, do you?' he murmured, before capturing her sob of surrender, in a possessive kiss.

Stop kissing him back!

Lacey tried to prevent her tongue from duelling with his, tried to close her lips against the delicious invasion, tried to ignore the onslaught of sensation charging through her body. But as Brandon's hands cradled her head, angling her mouth for better access, the desperate objections were incinerated in a new tidal wave of need.

The madness returned, rippling through her body and making every pulse-point ache.

The buzz of something against her chest duelled with the hammering thud of her heartbeat. But then she recognised the intermittent vibrations, enough to drag her lips from his.

'My-my phone…?' she stammered, trying to get her mind to engage.

He released her abruptly.

Panic arrived hot on the heels of desire. How could she have succumbed to him again, been so willing to throw herself back into the inferno?

The frown on his face did nothing to cover the heat and purpose in his gaze.

'I need to answer it…' she said, finally gathering enough of her wits to welcome the interruption. She scrambled to open her purse and locate the buzzing phone. But, when she saw her sister Milly's number, panic turned to raw terror.

Ruby?

She turned away from Brandon to accept the call. 'Milly, what is it? Is everything okay?'

'Hey, sis.' Milly's voice came down the line, dousing Lacey's foolish hormones in a bucket of icy water. 'Don't panic. It's just Rubes has woken up with a slight temperature.'

'What?' Panic turned to guilt and remorse and every molecule of shame in between. 'How high is it?'

'Honestly, it's not that bad. I've called the NHS helpline and they're calling me back… Oh, I'm so sorry,' Milly added. 'It's only five o'clock. Did I wake you up? I should have just texted you.'

'No, it's fine, Milly, I'll get the next train home from Gare du Nord.'

It was what she'd intended to do anyway, before she'd been waylaid by Brandon Cade…and an apology she had never expected. Followed by a mind-blowing kiss she totally should have declined.

She gripped the phone, suddenly remembering the man was listening to every word. Had she mentioned Ruby's name?

'Honestly, sis, you don't have to come home. You

should stay and enjoy yourself.' Milly's voice lifted with excitement. 'I saw the pics last night on the Internet. You looked fabulous, by the way. Where did you get that dress? And how the heck did you get an invite to the Durand Ball from Brandon Cade? I thought you were just interviewing him.'

'Um, I told you, it's a work assignment.' She interrupted Milly's stream of consciousness. Milly didn't know Cade was Ruby's father. No one knew. But Milly did know she had been dismissed from her job at Cade Inc when she'd got pregnant.

'Well, I hope you told him about the crappy way his HR department treated you?' Milly said, then chuckled. 'Although, to be fair, I don't think I'd have wanted to talk shop with him either. He is flipping gorgeous.'

'Right, Milly.' She sighed, her neck prickling at the thought Cade was listening to everything. 'I need to go, so I can pack and get to the station. And I should get off the phone in case the doctor is trying to call back.' She wanted to quiz Milly about her daughter's condition, but she didn't want to mention Ruby's name in front of Cade.

A sick feeling dropped into her stomach as she ended the call.

She'd created this situation with all her lies and evasions. Her decision not to tell Cade the truth five years ago. And all her bad choices in the last twelve hours.

She stuffed the phone into her bag with shaking fingers. He stood with his hands shoved into the pockets of his sweat pants, observing her with an intensity which only made the guilt and panic more acute.

'I really do have to go now,' she said.

He nodded. 'Who's Milly?'

'She's my sister, and she's not well,' she said, hating herself even more for yet another lie. 'I need to get back to London.'

He didn't challenge the latest lie and her panic eased. She hadn't mentioned Ruby during the call, or he surely would have asked who she was too.

But, even as the relief washed over her, the nausea in her gut churned. She would have to tell Brandon Cade of his daughter's existence. Not today. Ruby's illness was a reprieve of sorts—not least from their latest insane kiss. But she would have to tell him soon.

She'd had no right to keep Ruby from him. All the reasons for her continued silence had collapsed in the last half hour like a pack of dominoes. Especially once she'd discovered he had never intentionally destroyed her career.

She hadn't wanted to accept his apology at first, hadn't even wanted to believe it was sincere. But she'd been hopelessly naïve to believe he'd even cared about her enough to go to the trouble of having her blacklisted.

What on earth had she been expecting from him all those years ago? A declaration of undying love after a half-hour hook-up in a nightclub office?

She could see now her decision never to tell him

about his child had been cowardly, spiteful and wrong, on so many levels.

She still had no idea how he would react to the news. It was possible he would not want to acknowledge Ruby. He might also accuse her of using her child to extort money out of him… But telling Brandon Cade the truth wasn't really about how he would react, but what Ruby deserved.

Something she had never acknowledged.

Ruby deserved to have a father who knew about her existence. And a mother who didn't shy away from the tough choices because of her own cowardice.

Once she returned to London—and made sure her baby was okay—she was going to face up to all the consequences of that night, the way she should have faced up to them five years ago.

'You're close to your sister?' he asked with a curious expression on his face—not so much scepticism as confusion.

'Yes, very,' she said. At least that wasn't a lie.

She scooped her heels up off the carpet where she'd dropped them during their clinch. Humiliation washed over her again, as she slipped on the jewelled slippers, at the thought of how close she'd come to sleeping with him again. Of giving in to desire and letting his touch, his taste, his demands override all her priorities.

'I'll see myself out,' she said, and made a dash for the door.

He didn't try to stop her. Perhaps he had come to his senses about their latest moment of madness too.

She swallowed down the stupid lump of regret as she headed down the corridor to her own suite. The next time she saw Brandon, she needed to be in a lot better control of herself. So she could do the right thing at last for her little girl.

Twenty minutes later, though, as Lacey dashed into the hotel lobby, having showered and changed into the power suit she'd worn the day before, she discovered nothing was ever simple where Brandon Cade was concerned.

Because the man stood waiting for her.

'Brandon?' she said, her colour heightening. 'I… Hi.'

'Hello, Lacey.' Turning to the eager assistant standing behind him, he indicated the garment bag she carried. 'Take Ms Carstairs' bag to the heliport, and tell Jim we'll be ready to take off in ten minutes.'

'Wait? What?' Lacey stared, wide-eyed, as the garment bag—containing clothes which didn't even belong to her—was whisked out of her hand and the assistant headed for the lift, clearly all too eager to do his master's bidding.

Unlike Lacey.

'I have the helicopter waiting to take us back to Cade Tower in London,' he announced, cupping her elbow to direct her towards the lifts. 'My car can take you to your sister from there. Is she in hospital?'

Us.

The single word reverberated in Lacey's chest, disturbing her almost as much as the thought of spending several more hours in Brandon's company. Or the thought of the big reveal in their future which she was not remotely prepared for.

'No, Milly's at our flat, she's not that sick,' she sputtered as the lift shot towards the roof, and the feel of his fingers on her arm did all sorts of disturbing things to her equilibrium.

'You live with your sister?' he asked, then his lips quirked in that predatory smile which had disturbed her so much the day before. It wasn't doing much to calm her erratic heartbeat now either.

'Yes, we share a flat in Hackney,' she said, then realised she'd accidentally given him the location of her home. Her and Ruby's home, as well as Milly's. But, before she had a chance to kick herself, his smile widened.

'How gratifying,' he said.

She frowned, not sure what she was supposed to make of the smile now, because it almost looked possessive, as well as smug.

'Really, Milly's not that sick. I totally overreacted,' she added, determined to head him off at the pass—now that her worries about Ruby had been alleviated.

She had called Milly back after her shower to quiz her about Ruby's condition and her sister had confirmed the doctor had called and, after ruling out anything worrying, had told Milly to give Ruby a dose of children's painkiller. Milly had re-checked

Ruby's temperature at Lacey's request and it had already come down several degrees.

Unfortunately, her concerns about Brandon Cade were galloping off in the opposite direction with the speed of a runaway horse.

The guilt, which had been pushing at her chest ever since she'd left his suite, thundered under her breastbone as the lift glided to the hotel's rooftop heliport.

'Nevertheless, you are returning to London?' Brandon clarified.

'Yes, but…'

'Then it makes sense to take the chopper—it will be quicker.'

'But I really don't want to put you to all that trouble,' she said, getting a little frantic as all her lies threatened to choke her.

She didn't want him to meet Ruby. Not until she was ready. And she definitely was not ready now.

He let out an indulgent laugh which did not help with her growing anxiety at all.

'It's a little late for that, don't you think, Lacey?'

Ten minutes later, as the chopper lifted into the sky and Paris' Golden Triangle dropped away beneath them both, Lacey's stomach plummeted.

'I'm sorry, Mr Cade, the driver is on his way back from the Cade Estate, where you were due to arrive from Paris this afternoon.' The assistant at the London heliport glanced at his phone. 'We contacted him as soon as we heard about your change of plans, so he should arrive in approximately half an hour.'

Brandon frowned at the news.

'It's really okay, Brandon,' Lacey jumped in as they entered the lift together. 'I can catch a cab home. I really appreciate all you've done already,' she added, the relief on her face confusing him.

He wasn't buying the news her sister was okay, because he'd sensed her anxiety as she'd sat opposite him during the helicopter ride from Paris. He hadn't tried to engage her in too much conversation. Not only had it been difficult with the headsets on, but the only thing he really wanted to talk about was his plans for her... For *them*. And even he knew now wasn't the time.

He had planned to have his driver take her home to her sister, to give himself time to regroup and work out a strategy.

He wanted Lacey Carstairs to become his mistress. She was smart, engaging and prepared to stand up to him. And their sexual chemistry was off the charts. But he'd never dated anyone long term, just ask Misty. And he did not intend to embark on something he couldn't control. And at the moment his emotions where Lacey was concerned were a lot more volatile than he was accustomed to. She pushed buttons he had not even realised he had. And there was also the question of their past to handle—which was another novelty.

But, as he punched the button for the basement

garage on the lift panel, he found he was reluctant to let her out of his sight.

'It's not a problem, I have several cars here,' he said, deciding not to second-guess his concern on this occasion. It made sense not to let her go until they had agreed a time to meet again. 'I'll drive you home myself.'

'Really, Brandon, there's no need,' she said again, becoming almost frantic.

The lift doors swished open on the parking garage. The garage concierge, who had been waiting for them, handed him a key fob.

'The Mercedes is fuelled and waiting in Bay Six, Mr Cade,' the man informed him.

'What's the address?' he asked Lacey, taking her elbow again to direct her to the hybrid sports car. Tension rippled through her as they reached the bay.

'Seriously, Brandon, I can catch a cab.'

The car doors unlocked automatically. He sighed as she stood stubbornly beside the vehicle.

Where was that mulish expression coming from? Because he was beginning to suspect her stubbornness was more to do with a desire to get away from him than anything to do with her sister's health issues.

She still wanted him, so why was she so determined to push him away?

'We can either have a stand-off, or you can give me the address. Your choice.'

Her brows lowered. 'Okay, fine. But I'm not going to invite you in,' she said.

He opened the passenger door and she climbed into the car. At last. 'I don't recall asking you to,' he said, strapping himself into the driver's seat.

He had no desire to meet her sister. He was not remotely interested in her domestic situation, other than the gratifying discovery she was not currently dating anyone. But then, he hadn't expected her to be. There was something strangely innocent about Lacey Carstairs even now—five years after he'd been her first lover—which convinced him she was not the kind of woman who would sleep with more than one man at a time.

And, although he did not like the thought she must have slept with several other men in the intervening years, the sweetness of the girl he'd once known which still clung to her was another big point in her favour. Why he should find it so, he had no idea, because innocence—or even the suggestion of innocence—had never appealed to him before. But again, maybe it was simply Lacey's novelty value.

'Okay, as long as that's understood,' she said, finally relaxing enough to reel off an address in East London. 'I don't want Milly meeting you and putting two and two together to make five hundred,' she added, as he keyed her address into the car's GPS.

The device estimated a drive time of thirty minutes—past the Tower of London, through the City and then along the leafy Georgian terraces of Islington before they reached their destination in an up-and-coming neighbourhood he had never visited before. The car purred to life and he headed out of the garage into the morning sunshine and across London Bridge.

Thirty minutes was all the time he needed, he decided, to steamroller over all her objections and get her back in his bed, ASAP.

'What did you mean, your sister would put two and two together and make five hundred?'

Lacey glanced over at the man she had been trying to ignore ever since she had been forced to climb into his luxury car twenty minutes ago. The question seemed innocuous. But there was nothing innocuous about Brandon Cade. And she was just now beginning to come to terms with that. Her abject panic, as his powerful muscle car cruised through the empty streets of white stucco-fronted Georgian terraces in Islington towards a date with destiny, not so much.

If only she could have texted Milly, ensured she didn't bring Ruby out of the flat to greet them when they arrived—however slight the chance—she might have been able to stop freaking out. But how could she text her sister when Brandon was sitting right beside her, his intense, all-seeing gaze flicking between her and the road?

'I just meant, she'd totally assume we were dating,' she replied, knowing her sister's misconceptions about her love life were the least of her worries. 'Milly's a hopeless romantic and she saw the photos of us last night at the ball. You'd probably be subjected to a half-hour inquisition on your intentions,' she panic-babbled. 'And you've spent more than enough time and money dealing with my family issues already this morning…' The panic babble finally hit a dead end.

'Interesting. I never would have guessed you'd be quite so concerned about disrupting the schedule of an arrogant, overbearing half-wit like myself,' he mused, sending her a half-smile which made it clear he was teasing her.

She might have found his mockery disarming—might even have been able to see the funny side of the situation—if only she wasn't so hyper-aware of the height, breadth and precariousness of the house of cards she had constructed over five years…

Even though Brandon was unlikely to meet his daughter today—Ruby would surely still be sleeping?—sweat crawled down her back like the fingers of a corpse.

Brandon had been charming and thoughtful, as well as annoyingly forceful in his determination to take her home—which only made the lies she'd told him, and last night's booty call, all the more damning.

'I'm sorry I called you that,' she said, her contrition complete. Maybe he had deserved it once, but did he really deserve it now? Given all the things she'd kept from him? 'I apologise.'

'Don't apologise,' he said, surprising her again. 'I'm sure my business rivals will attest to the fact I'm not a halfwit, but overbearing and arrogant probably aren't far off the mark. I blame my over-privileged and entitled upbringing myself,' he said with a harsh laugh, which made her wonder exactly how privileged his upbringing had really been.

She knew, because she'd read everything she could about him once upon a time, that he had grown up in the sole care of his father after his parents' acrimonious divorce when he'd been only a few months old. He had never wanted for anything, materially speaking, his father having become a media baron long before Brandon—his only child—had been born. But she had often wondered what it must have been like growing up in the care of paid caregivers and in a string of exclusive boarding schools with no mother, no siblings and a father who must have been absent a lot of the time.

'That's very reasonable of you,' she managed, disturbed all over again by how accommodating he was being.

'I thought so,' he said. She huffed out a strained laugh, realising, however accommodating Brandon was, he would always want the last word.

The car drove past the park where she often took Ruby to play at the weekend. And the guilt came barrelling back.

Then he took another turn onto the street where she lived with their child.

'Which one is yours?' he asked as the GPS announced they had reached their destination.

She pointed at the Victorian terrace where her flat was situated, glad to see no small face at the window.
Ruby is still in bed. Thank God.
But as he braked and she unhooked her seatbelt,

frantic to see her daughter and get away from the emotions threatening to overwhelm her, his warm hand landed on her knee.

'I want to see you again, Lacey. And soon,' he declared.

'What?' she yelped, the purpose in his gaze almost as terrifying as the blaze of heat at her core. And the elated leap in her heartrate.

'Come on, you can't be that surprised?' he said, the quirk of his lips suggesting he found her shock amusing. 'Given the intensity of our connection last night?' His land lifted off her knee to stroke her cheek, the rush of sensation as devastating as it was shocking. 'And the way we both went off like firecrackers five years ago?'

Just get out of the car, Lace. You have to get out of the car.

But somehow the instruction wouldn't compute. Her emotions were in turmoil again—her guilt and remorse as volatile as the need and the strange, idiotic joy. Because he wanted her.

'You excite me, Lacey, in a way no woman has for far too long,' he said, cupping her chin to lift her face. 'This kind of sexual chemistry is extremely rare.' She blinked, aware of the pheromones firing through her system alongside the panic. And that desperate, bone-sapping need to have him kiss her.

Almost as if he'd sensed her need, her yearning, his mouth took hers in a punishing, possessive kiss. She responded—because of course she did. She couldn't seem to resist him.

He tore his mouth free. 'Once you have satisfied yourself your sister is well, we should speak. Soon. How about I call you tonight?'

She couldn't think. Couldn't respond. Her lips were still buzzing from his kiss. Her brain whirring in about a thousand different directions. The yearning in his eyes was almost as devastating as the responding yearning in her heart.

But, before she could come up with a coherent answer, his gaze shifted to something behind her. 'Is that your sister?' he asked. 'You didn't tell me she had a child.'

She shifted round to see Milly walking down the steps of the house towards them with Ruby in her arms, bouncing up and down.

Every molecule of blood drained from her head to slam into her heart as she scrambled out of the car.

No. No. No. Please no. Not now. Not like this.

As Milly and Ruby approached her, Milly's words seemed to come from a million miles away.

'Ruby wanted to come out and greet you. Her temp's back to normal and she's been waiting for you.' Her sister's gaze shifted to the muscle car parked at the kerb. 'Oh. My. God.' She whispered. 'That's him, isn't it? He brought you home. That's so romantic.' She grinned. Lacey heard a car door slam and footsteps—firm, inexorable—hitting the pavement behind her.

She stood frozen, her whole body going hot and cold and then hot again, the panic reaching fever pitch. The guilt choked her. Her daughter's arms lifted towards her, but it was as if Lacey were in the midst of a dream. A terrible anxiety dream, each awful aspect of which was unfolding in agonising slow motion.

Her daughter's smile spread over her face, her mouth forming the first word she had ever learned to say as Lacey was wrenched out of the dream and plunged into cold, hard reality.

'Mummy! Mummy! Mummy! You're home.'

CHAPTER SIX

THE CHILD IS LACEY'S?

Brandon stared in disbelief as the woman he had just spent an incendiary night with, the woman he had been determined to make his mistress, scooped the round-faced little girl out of her sister's arms.

Why didn't she tell me she has a child?

Shock was swiftly followed by suspicion and a wary, strangely emotional, tension in his gut as he watched the child sling her arms around Lacey's neck… Her mother's neck… And begin to chatter as if her life depended on it.

Lacey, though, remained tense, her smile strained even as she greeted her daughter with effusive praise.

He couldn't move as he struggled to process this unprecedented new reality. But then all the opportunities she'd had over the last twenty-four hours to inform him she had a child occurred to him. Suspicion writhed in his gut. Something wasn't right here, he knew that much, but he could not seem to grasp what. And he hated that.

But then the little girl's babbling stopped and her bright gaze landed on him.

'Who is that man, Mummy? Is he your friend?' she asked.

Brandon tensed at the innocent question, feeling oddly exposed but not sure why. Lacey glanced over her shoulder again, her reluctance to introduce him to her daughter abundantly clear.

Confused and still stunned by this development, Brandon added irritation to the mix.

She should have told him she was a mother, but he didn't see how that changed anything. He still wanted her. Anything could be negotiated, if he was willing to be flexible, and it surprised him—and annoyed him a little—to realise that, to have her, he could be flexible even about this. If this responsibility was why she had been so surprised at his offer—perhaps believing he wouldn't have wanted her if he'd known—he could at least disabuse her of that fact.

So, as she hesitated, he stepped forward. 'Yes, I'm a friend of your mother's,' he said to the girl. 'My name is Brandon Cade,' he added, not really sure how one addressed a child.

The child giggled. 'Hello, my name's Ruby,' she said with a boldness which reminded him of her mother. As she grinned, the emerald green of her eyes sparkled with delight and a dimple appeared in her left cheek.

Something odd struck him right in the solar plexus. A strange sense of *déjà vu*. Of familiarity. Almost as if he'd seen this child before.

He shook his head slightly, trying to shake the disorientating feeling loose.

'Hi, I'm Milly Devlin, Lacey's sister. It's so nice to meet you at last,' the other woman said, holding out her hand.

Brandon shook it, noting the similarities between the two women. And the fact her sister looked perfectly okay. 'Hello, I'm glad to see you are fully recovered,' he said, the suspicion turning into a hole in his gut. A large black hole. Especially when the sister sent him a puzzled look.

'Oh, it wasn't me who was ill, it was Rubes,' she offered. She stroked a hand down her niece's hair. 'But you're all better now, aren't you?'

'But I can't go to school today, can I, Mummy? Please, Mummy, I want to stay home with you and Milly,' the little girl said, the grin disappearing as she grasped Lacey's cheeks and sent her mother a winsome, pleading look that would have persuaded a stone.

'Yes, you can stay home today, Rubes.' She glanced at Brandon at last. And he spotted the shadow of guilt in her eyes. 'We should go inside. Thanks so much for driving me home, Brandon.'

She headed into the house with her daughter before he could reply. Her sister waved goodbye and followed.

But as he stood there on the pavement, watching the little girl and her mother disappear, he couldn't seem to move, couldn't seem to think.

The boa constrictor in his gut coiled and clenched

into a tight knot. At last he forced himself to return to his car, but as he drove away from the house on the leafy lane the knot swelled and twisted.

Why had Lacey lied about her sister's health? About the existence of her daughter?

And then a new question struck him. And his breath seized.

Ruby went to school. Exactly how old was the little girl?

He stared blankly at the road ahead. After stopping at some traffic lights, he engaged the car's hands-free phone and tapped through to his executive assistant, his fingers trembling.

'Daryl, Lacey Carstairs has a daughter. I want you to find out when the child was born, and if there's a father listed on the birth certificate.'

But as he signed off, and continued to drive back towards the City, it felt as if he were driving into a fog. Because he could already feel the bomb, which Lacey had armed with her silence, about to explode right in the middle of his carefully ordered life.

'What is going on between you and the extremely fit media mogul?' Milly's gaze narrowed on Lacey's face.

'Nothing,' Lacey lied, busy filling a saucepan with water so she could prepare lunch. She'd already had an inquisition from her editor, who had allowed her to spend the day at home to write the piece on the Durand Ball. But what on earth could she write that was fit to print?

Not meeting Milly's gaze was a mistake. She'd never been good at lying to her sister.

'She has his eyes, you know,' Milly said softly.

Lacey spun round, splashing water over her wrist. 'What?' she said, but she could already see the game was up. Because Milly was looking at her with a devastating mix of sympathy and concern.

'No wonder you were so nervous about going to interview him,' Milly mused. 'I thought it was because it was such a big opportunity for you. And, well, he's him,' she added as Lacey's anxiety shot back towards the danger zone—a level it had been hovering around ever since Brandon Cade had introduced himself to his own daughter half an hour ago, and that puzzled expression had crossed his face as he'd got a good look at Ruby.

Lacey's stomach plummeted back to her toes and kept on going.

Milly turned off the tap, the water having overflowed the saucepan. She lifted the pan out of Lacey's numb fingers and placed it on the sideboard.

'He's Ruby's dad, isn't he?' she said.

The question reverberated in Lacey's soul.

And suddenly she couldn't hold the lie in any longer. Not from her sister, not even from herself. And so she nodded.

Milly swore softly. 'And I'm taking it he doesn't know?'

Lacey shook her head, the sting of tears hurting her eyes. Tears of self-pity which she had no right to shed. 'I think he probably does now. Or he will figure it out,' she said, then let the breath out which had been clogged in her lungs for hours.

She had absolutely no idea how long it would take Brandon to figure out the truth. Or what he was likely to do with the knowledge. But one thing she did know, he would not go easy on her.

She had blindsided him. Taken something from him she had no right to take. Whether he wanted to be a father or not, he was one. And he had been one for four years and three months.

She blinked, then scrubbed away the errant tear that trickled down her cheek. What was worse, she wasn't sure any more she deserved to have him go easy on her.

'Did something happen between you two last night too?' Milly asked.

Lacey's gaze darted to Milly's, her cheeks exploding with heat.

'I thought he looked rather possessive when he came striding out of that amazing car,' Milly murmured.

Lacey groaned. When exactly had she become so transparent?

'I'm so sorry I brought Ruby out with me,' Milly said, clearly picking up on Lacey's panic and distress.

'Don't be,' Lacey said, finally looking her sister square in the eye. 'You didn't do anything wrong.' And neither had Brandon Cade. Not yet, anyway. 'I should have told him about Ruby yesterday.' She swore under her breath, a word she hadn't used in years. 'The truth is, I should have told him about her when she was born.'

'Why should you have done that?' Milly said forcefully, always willing to offer support, even when Lacey knew she didn't deserve it. 'Ruby is happy and healthy. She has a good home and we love her. That's no small feat, considering how little support we got from Dad after Mum died.'

'Ruby also doesn't have a father,' Lacey said. 'And that's on me.'

'Well, maybe now she does,' Milly offered, always determined to look on the bright side. 'And the guy's a drop-dead gorgeous gazillionaire who appears to still be into you. So, that has to be good for something.'

'Except I don't think he's going to be into me any more,' Lacey said, fairly sure it would be better if he wasn't, because this situation was already catastrophic enough without factoring in the sexual chemistry, which made her do stupid things. 'And I have no idea how he's going to react.' Just thinking about all the things he might do was making her stomach hurt. 'What if he tries to take Ruby from me?'

'He won't,' Milly said with a cast-iron confidence Lacey knew was at best optimistic, and at worst totally misplaced.

Brandon Cade was a powerful man, and she knew he also had the ability to be incredibly ruthless.

If only she'd thought of that last night, when she

had fallen to pieces in his arms for the second time in her life.

'But perhaps you should tell him the truth now, instead of waiting for him to find out,' Milly said.

Lacey nodded. Her sister was right. How could she fight for Ruby's best interests if she didn't even have the guts to face the man who had fathered her? She had to get out ahead of this situation now and stop hiding.

But as Milly took over lunch duties, and Lacey walked into the flat's small hallway to call Brandon's assistant—because she didn't even have his private number—her phone dinged.

She read the email from Daryl Wilson and the fear, which she had hoped finally to get a handle on, returned full-force.

Ms Carstairs, I have attached the solicitor's letter which I am sending via courier today to demand a DNA test of your minor child, Ruby Devlin Carstairs—who Mr Cade has reason to believe may be his biological daughter. Once the DNA test is completed, Mr Cade's legal team will arrange a meeting to discuss the results of the test and how their client intends to proceed in this matter. Feel free to contact me if you have any questions.

Lacey pressed a hand to her mouth, her fingers shaking as she scanned the contents of the letter Brandon's assistant had attached. Like the email, it was cold, clinical, demanding and totally devoid of feeling, almost as if each carefully chosen syllable had been steeped in Brandon's anger.

The musical jingle from Ruby's cartoon started to play in the next room, the notes light and airy and innocent, accompanied by the joyous, uncomplicated sound of her little girl's laughter... And in direct contrast to the suffocating feeling dragging at Lacey's insides.

She'd taken too long, been too much of a coward, and now her little girl could well be forced to pay the price.

CHAPTER SEVEN

'MR CADE, MS CARSTAIRS has arrived, are you ready for her?' Daryl asked, peering around the office door as he addressed Brandon and the four solicitors who he had been discussing next steps with for two hours.

Brandon glared at his assistant.

No, I'll never be ready for this.

The words he wanted to speak echoed in his skull, alongside the anger that had been building steadily for the last three days, ever since he'd laid eyes on Ruby Devlin Carstairs. The anger that had surged yesterday when he had read the DNA test report he'd had commissioned once Daryl had got back to him with the details of the child's birth certificate.

Lacey's child had been born thirty-eight weeks and three days after he had made wild, passionate love to her in the manager's office of a Soho night-club. When she had been a virgin, and the condom he had worn had split.

Dammit. Not just Lacey's child. My child.

The father had been unlisted on the birth certificate.

Just one more injustice to add to all the others.

He raked his fingers over his scalp. And took a deep breath, trying to steady the emotions which had been tying his guts into knots ever since discovering there was a ninety-nine-point-eight percent probability he was Ruby Carstairs' biological father. Not that he'd really needed the confirmation.

Because he'd known somehow she was his as soon as he'd looked into her eyes and seen the same dark green as his own.

Lacey had lied to him for five years. And had made him a worse man than his father.

He had never planned to have children. Never even contemplated it. For the simple reason he was fairly sure he did not have the sensibilities to nurture or protect a child. But it was way too late to worry about that now.

He had to deal with what was, not what should have been.

Ruby Devlin Carstairs was a part of him. And, however angry he was with her mother for keeping her existence from him—however angry he was with himself, for not checking on Lacey after that long-ago encounter—he could not abandon the child…the way his own mother had abandoned him.

How the hell he formed a relationship with this child, he had no idea. He knew absolutely nothing about children. But one thing was certain, her mother would no longer be calling the shots.

'Sure, show her in,' he said, then stalked round to stand behind his desk and stare out at the morning skyline.

He forced himself to keep breathing, to stop his temper from exploding. The prickle of aware-ness—dammit, of arousal—rushing over his skin only made his control shakier as he turned to watch her enter the room.

She wore a similar outfit to the one she'd worn less than a week ago. In his office. When he hadn't known who she was. And she *had* known he was the father of her child. Demure, tempting, torment-ing. But now the glimpse of cleavage, the heightened colour on her face and the shadows in her eyes only made the fury worse—because arousal exploded too.

He still wanted her. Even though she had deceived him for five years.

John Marrow, the head of his legal team, got the meeting started then launched into the first order of business.

'As you know, Ms Carstairs, the DNA test results we received yesterday afternoon confirm Mr Cade, our client, is the biological father of your daughter Ruby Devlin Carstairs.'

'Yes.' Her soft acknowledgement made his shoul-ders tighten, the anger gripping his insides. 'I know.'

The fury exploded, but right beneath it were so many other emotions he couldn't control and didn't want to name.

He braced himself against the wave of fury and glared at her.

'How long?' he snarled, the other people in the room fading from his consciousness, because all he could see was her.

'Mr Cade, I'm not sure that…' Marrow began.

'How long have you known she was mine?' he demanded, ignoring the solicitor's interruption, focussed only on Lacey.

She flinched, but her gaze remained direct, her tone flat. 'As soon as I discovered I was pregnant.'

'You bitch,' he snapped.

Marrow and his team stiffened in unison, but Lacey didn't flinch again, she simply stared back, as if she was absorbing his anger, his anguish. Which only made the emotions harder to control, the temper searing his insides now like a wildfire threatening to burn through the last of his composure.

'What gave you the right to keep my child's existence from me?'

'Mr Cade, I really don't think…' Marrow began again.

'Shut up and leave,' Brandon said, casting a searing glance at the man and his team. 'I want to speak to her alone.'

The rest of the legal team immediately packed up their briefcases, but Marrow hesitated. 'Mr Cade, you're not yourself. I don't think…'

'It's okay, Mr Marrow,' Lacey said, her gaze still locked on his, still calm, still stoic, but for the quivers running through her body. 'He won't hurt me.'

'If you're sure, Ms Carstairs?' Marrow said, but as soon as Lacey nodded the solicitor was out the door in ten seconds flat.

Brandon might have admired her courage, ex-

cept he was still so angry with her, he could hardly
see straight.

He stalked around the desk, bearing down on her,
wanting to see her flinch, wanting her to see how
angry he was. 'How do you know I won't hurt you?'

'Because you already did, and I survived,' she
said, standing up, refusing to be cowed, the storm
in her eyes matching the storm raging in his heart.

He had vowed, a long time ago, he would never
give another woman the power to hurt him the way
the mother he'd only met once had hurt him. But
somehow this woman had slipped under his radar.

Right from the first moment he'd met her, she'd
made him feel more, want more. And now here he
was, being forced to pay the price for those moments
of weakness. The fact he still wanted her only added
insult to that madness.

'How did *I* hurt *you*?' He spat the question at her.
But, instead of getting the litany of pathetic excuses
for her deception he'd been expecting, she drew in a
heavy breath. And broke eye contact.

'It doesn't matter,' she said. 'I'm not here to make
excuses for what I did. I'm here to apologise and to
make amends. If that's possible.' He didn't believe
the contrite act—why the hell should he?—but, before he could formulate a suitably scathing response,
her gaze returned to his. 'You can punish me all you
want, but one thing I won't let you do is punish Ruby.
None of this is her fault.'

'True, I think we can both agree it's your fault,'
he shot back. But, instead of arguing and giving him

the satisfaction of slapping her down *again*, the shadows in her eyes intensified.

She nodded. But her easy acceptance only annoyed him more. Where did she get off, playing the martyr?

He grasped her arm, tugged her towards him, the sizzle of heat electrifying. And not in a good way.

'So you admit, you deserve to be punished?' he said, just to be clear. He was not sure where the hell he was going with this, but knew he needed to establish control.

She tugged her arm free and rubbed her bicep, her eyes flaring with the fierce passion he had always found so irresistible.

By now he ought to find it repellent. Unfortunately, nothing could be further from the truth.

'I didn't say that,' she said. 'But, if retribution is what you require, I can live with it. Just please don't hurt my daughter.'

He blinked and stepped back, the look of genuine fear on her face like a bucket of ice thrown over the wildfire burning in his stomach.

He swore under his breath, then marched back towards the window to stare out at the host of London landmarks looking proud and indomitable in the sunshine. The Victorian majesty of Tower Bridge in the distance, the Baroque splendour of St Paul's Cathedral's dome nestled among the harsh modern geometric shapes of newer developments on the opposite bank of the river... Several agonising seconds passed as he struggled to regain the cast-iron control—which he'd just lost so comprehensively.

What was happening to him? He had intended to be ruthless, determined and, most of all, composed. Instead of which he'd behaved like a petulant bully. He was angry with her, and he had every right to be, but he had never intended to make her fear for the child.

'I think you mean *our* child, don't you?' he managed at last. Resentment still edged his tone, but underneath he sensed the reason for his spectacular loss of control.

Panic.

For the first time in his life, he had no strategy, no plan. He had no idea how to be a father, or if he even wanted to be one. And whatever he decided he knew he would need her help—which only made this situation more untenable.

He had never relied on anyone, had never trusted anyone since he'd been a little boy, and he'd learned not to trust.

And now he would have to rely on a woman who had lied to him for five years—whose effect on him he still had no damn control over—to show him how to be a parent to a child he did not know. And did not know how to get to know.

Terrific.

Lacey breathed through the anxiety as the hard line of Brandon's shoulders softened just a little.

She drew in a careful breath, easing the painful vice around her ribs which had been tightening ever since she'd received the text from his assistant three days ago.

She'd been scared of what would happen at this meeting, what he might demand, and the team of lawyers hadn't exactly put her at ease. She'd assumed he would be cold, clinical, frighteningly controlled. His visible fury, his loss of control, had shocked her to her core.

'Yes, our child,' she said, trying desperately to form some kind of connection with him. To reach out and soothe.

Stupid, really, that she should feel any sympathy for him. He was her enemy now in a lot of ways, and an extremely formidable enemy at that. It was obvious he was furious with her, and she'd been going over and over in her head all the possible ways he could make her pay for her five years of silence.

But, despite her fear, there was something about his volatile response which felt familiar, almost reassuring in a weird way. Because it reminded her of her own panic—at the enormity of the task now facing her—when the two clear red lines had appeared on the pregnancy test kit.

Somehow Brandon's temper—his tenuous hold on his emotions—felt better than the clinical indifference of his solicitor's letter and the communications she'd had since about Ruby, all filtered through his assistant. She'd been terrified Ruby's existence would mean nothing to him—other than a means to punish her for defying him—but that, at least, did not seem to be the case.

He huffed and shoved his hands into his trouser pockets, still staring at the staggering view of the London skyline, his back turned to her.

'It's not my intention to hurt her,' he said, his tone clipped and still edged with bitterness, but she could hear the weariness too.

Was it possible he had struggled as much as she once had with the thought of becoming a parent?

Of course it is.

The guilt she'd tried to ignore dropped back into her stomach like a stone.

And he hasn't had eight months to prepare, the way you did. Because you denied him that chance.

'It was wrong of me to keep her a secret from you,' she said again. Seeing his back muscles tense, she had to force herself to continue. 'I persuaded myself it was in her best interests. Once I'd decided to have her, I convinced myself you wouldn't want her, wouldn't even want me to have her, that you'd put pressure on me not to.'

He swung round, his brows flattening. 'You thought I'd force you to have an abortion?' he said. 'On what evidence, for God's sake?'

'From what you said *that* night… After…after we made her…' She stuttered to a stop, the fierce expression making her feel like that naïve intern again.

'What did I say?' he asked.

'You said it shouldn't have happened. That the condom had split, and if there were consequences to contact your office so you could deal with it.' She repeated his words almost verbatim, because she'd never forgotten them. They had been etched on her memory like a wound.

He pressed his lips together—as if he doubted her recollection. It seemed what he'd said to her that night had not been etched on *his* memory. But then he leaned back against his desk, crossed his arms over his chest and dropped his searing gaze from her face. He swore softly. Uncrossing his arms, he shoved his hands back into his pockets, his gaze locking on hers again.

'I don't remember saying that, but I wouldn't be surprised if I did. I was still reeling from the shock of discovery you were a virgin and that I had taken you with such…urgency.'

She nodded, the grudging concession making her eyes sting—because it gave her some validation, for the girl she'd been. She had been young and foolish that night, but she hadn't been wrong about the intensity of their connection.

The steely light in his eyes hardened. 'Although, none of that explains why you didn't tell me about the child when you came to interview me, or while we were at the ball or…' His gaze drifted down, making her aware of all the erogenous zones he had exploited a week ago. 'Before we slept together a second time. You had a ton of opportunities, and you didn't take them. Why?'

The vice around her ribs winched tight again. And it was her turn to fold her arms around her waist, trying to protect herself once again from that searing gaze.

'I should have said something. You're right,' she said, hoping he wouldn't take it any further.

'You'll have to do better than that, Lacey.'

Heat exploded in her cheeks, matched by the fierce heat lighting his gaze as he stepped closer. She inched back a step, only to have her legs hit the chair. She couldn't retreat any further.

'I guess I got distracted,' she managed.

'Still not good enough,' he said, pulling his hand out of his pocket. The purpose in his gaze became all-consuming as his thumb skimmed down her burning cheek.

Her breath hitched painfully, her senses going haywire as the light touch inched down to sweep across her collarbone and glide over the upper swell of her breast. But, unlike four nights ago, this time she found the strength to brush his hand away, no matter how much she still yearned for his touch. 'Don't touch me, Brandon, it doesn't help.'

But he only laughed, the gruff chuckle as bitter as it was commanding. 'Really?' he murmured. 'Your body says otherwise.'

'So what?' she said, determined to be the woman she'd become over the last five years—strong, smart, brave—instead of that foolish girl again.

This situation was more than complicated, and combustible enough without them stoking the madness. And succumbing to it again would only leave her more vulnerable. More at his mercy.

The sharp knock at the door had him finally breaking eye contact.

He swore and raked his fingers through his hair as Lacey wrapped her arms tightly around her midriff to hold in the throbbing ache, the devastating yearning.

Don't let him intimidate you or bring that girl out of hiding. Not again.

She sat, her knees turning to water as he stalked back behind his desk to sit down too.

'Mr Cade, there's been a development,' his assistant said as he rushed into the room.

'What development?' Brandon asked, and Daryl—usually so composed and professional—flushed, then handed him a smartphone.

'I just got this message from a reliable source at Drystar Media Group,' he said, mentioning a publishing company that Lacey knew owned a host of tabloid titles globally.

Brandon's expression tensed, his jaw hardening as Daryl continued. 'Apparently, they're going to run the story tomorrow across all their US titles.'

'How the hell did they get this information?' The suppressed rage in Brandon's voice made Lacey stiffen.

'I should go,' Lacey said, standing up, suddenly desperate to escape.

But, before she could move, Brandon's gaze flicked to her. 'Stay put,' he commanded in a strident tone which instantly put her back up. But then his gaze softened slightly. 'This concerns you too.'

What? How?

'We don't know. It may have been a leak at the DNA test facility,' Daryl supplied.

She collapsed back into the chair.

Drystar knew about Ruby? And they were going to publish a story about her child? The horrifying implications hit her.

She'd been concerned about how their lives would change now Brandon knew of his daughter's existence, but this…*this* could be so much worse. To have the details of her life, the circumstances of her child's birth, splashed all over the celebrity press, dissected and pawed over by every media outlet from here to Timbuktu…

'The angle they are going with is you as a deadbeat billionaire dad,' Daryl continued in a pragmatic tone. 'Who got a nineteen-year-old employee pregnant then fired her and refused to acknowledge her, let alone support his child.'

'But that's not true!' Lacey gasped.

Neither Brandon nor Daryl seemed to hear her.

'What else?' Brandon said, not even glancing her way.

'I spoke to Fiona in PR and Dan on the NA acquisitions team,' Daryl added. 'They both say it will sink the Atlanta deal, unless we get out ahead of it with an alternative narrative.'

Brandon nodded.

She could see his mind working, but had no idea what he was thinking as his gaze fixed back on her burning face.

'Why don't we just tell them the truth?' she offered. 'I can tell them you didn't know Ruby existed until three days ago.'

But he barely acknowledged her suggestion, instead turning to Daryl again. 'Get Marrow and the rest of the legal team back in here. And tell them we're going with Plan B.'

Lacey shifted in her chair, to give herself time to get her rampaging heartbeat under control as Daryl left the room. But, when she looked at Brandon, his expression had the panic clawing at her chest again like a wild dog. Because the volatile emotions on his face when she had first arrived, even the passion of moments ago, had disappeared, to be replaced with the same distant, determined and utterly ruthless expression which had devastated her five years ago.

'What's Plan B?' she managed, even though she suddenly felt as insecure and powerless as she had in that nightclub office.

The emerald fire in his eyes was shockingly explicit, but his tone was laced with ice. 'We get married.'

CHAPTER EIGHT

'YOU'RE NOT... YOU'RE not serious?' Lacey stammered, not sure she'd heard Brandon correctly as Daryl trooped back into the room with the legal team.

But, as the group took their seats, the only person she could focus on was Brandon, his calm expression suggesting he had just supplied a perfectly reasonable solution to their problem instead of something completely insane.

Her breathing accelerated, alongside her panicked heartbeat, though the meeting proceeded as if she were a ghost, invisible to everyone but herself.

Brandon's gaze raked over her, then landed on the head of his legal team. He began firing out orders as if he were the captain of a ship about to go to war.

Marrow, his team and Daryl jotted down the directives—everything from drafting a prenup to how to divide his property portfolio—on their phones and laptops.

'But I haven't agreed to marry you...!' Lacey at last managed to butt into the conversation.

What was going on? Because she felt as if she were on a rollercoaster which was careering out of control, a rollercoaster she'd never even agreed to ride…

But Brandon and the rest of the room ignored her. *Again.*

'Daryl, talk to Claire in finance.' Brandon turned to his assistant. 'Tell her to arrange a monthly allowance of five times Ms Carstairs' current salary. She can't work as a celebrity journalist for the foreseeable future. And tell her to arrange child support payments to cover all my daughter's expenses. We can set up trusts, college funds, et cetera at a later date. And I want her officially named as my heir. Ms Carstairs and my child can relocate to the Cade estate in Wiltshire until the wedding.'

Lacey's mind was reeling, her panic so huge now it was beginning to choke her, when Brandon added, 'I want to announce the engagement in a press release by 8:00 a.m. tomorrow morning UK time—so we can pre-empt the headlines in the US. Everyone got that?'

They all nodded, except Lacey, who had rollercoastered her way into an alternative universe. Was she imagining this?

She had no intention of marrying Brandon Cade, or giving up her job, or relocating to Wiltshire, for that matter. But then, he still hadn't actually asked her to do any of those things.

'Okay, thanks, now get moving—we have a lot to do,' he announced.

With that, they all filed back out of the room.

The door closed behind them, the muted thud drowned out by the frantic beat of Lacey's pulse as she stared, incredulously, at Brandon.

He rose and walked round the desk to stand in front of her.

She forced herself to stand too, despite the liquid in her knees. She pressed her arms to her sides and squeezed trembling fingers into tight fists until her knuckles whitened.

'Aren't you forgetting something fairly important?' she said at last, feeling utterly overwhelmed but determined not to show it.

One thing she had always known—if you let Brandon Cade see a weakness, he would exploit it.

He leaned against his desk and folded his arms across his chest. The arrogant half-smile she was starting to hate played on his lips—but there was no amusement in his eyes. 'And what would that be?'

'I haven't agreed to marry you. In fact, you haven't even asked me,' she said, finally grabbing hold of the righteous indignation which was her only defence against his unbelievable arrogance.

'I haven't asked you because this isn't a choice, for either one of us,' he said, the dimple disappearing as well as the half-smile—somehow the sober, serious expression was even more arrogant. 'Marriage is our only option.'

'For you, maybe,' she shot back, her temper finally arriving full force. 'I realise the angle Drystar are planning to run with on this is not going to be good for your image or your US deal. And I will do everything I can to mitigate that, by stating clearly and unequivocally you didn't know of Ruby's existence until three days ago.'

It would be a public humiliation, and she had no doubt at all there would be little or no sympathy for her behaviour from the keyboard warriors on social media. But maybe that was the punishment she deserved for allowing her own hurt and cowardice to get in the way of doing the right thing, not just five years ago but a week ago too.

'I realise this is my fault,' she continued. 'But I'm not about to give up a job I love, or uproot me and Ruby and Milly to move to Wiltshire, and become your convenient bride just so you can—'

'You little fool.' He straightened as the mask of arrogance dropped to be replaced by barely contained fury. 'Do you really think this is about saving the Atlanta deal?'

'Yes, I do,' she said boldly.

'Do you have any idea what your life and our daughter's life—even your sister's life, for that matter—is going to be like when this story breaks tomorrow?'

She stared at him. 'I'm sure it will be a little fraught for a while but—'

'*Fraught?*' he shouted, his tone laced with bitterness as well as fury. 'All three of you will become the epicentre of a media storm. A storm I've been in the eye of my entire life. And my child will be in the eye of that storm too. You think the fact she's still a toddler will make any difference? It won't. And I refuse to let that happen. She needs and deserves my protection. And that is exactly what she will get.'

'I see…' She tried to get her mind into gear. To take on board what he was saying, and to deal with the sudden leap in her heart rate at the evidence he cared about their daughter enough to protect her.

Why had she doubted that so readily?

'I can arrange for me and Ruby and Milly to stay with friends if we need to, but I can't marry you.'

She didn't want to be dependent on Brandon. But there were so many other reasons why marriage would be a bad idea. They didn't know each other… She wasn't even sure they liked each other that much. And what about Ruby? Yes, she deserved to know her father, and vice versa. But they didn't need to get married for that to happen. And, anyway, how would a marriage between them even work? Was he talking about a marriage of convenience? To stem the media coverage? Or something more *involved*…?

She swallowed heavily, her cheeks igniting again.

Because underneath all her other misgivings was the biggest one of all. What if that lonely, anxious, naïve girl came out of hiding again? The one who had been so desperate for his approval she had convinced herself she loved him after only one night, and been so devastated by his rejection? She couldn't be that girl again, not even a little bit. But she wasn't sure she could be entirely rational where Brandon Cade was concerned…

'The story will surely die down in a few weeks,' she tried again, suddenly desperate to avert the marriage. Because it felt like too much. Just like Brandon Cade had always been too much.

'If you absolutely insist, we could announce our engagement,' she added, trying to find some middle ground—after all, this situation was not Brandon's fault, and she wanted to be fair to him, or as fair as she could be. But she refused to be railroaded. 'To deflect attention and supply a new narrative for the press until it all blows over? And then we can quietly announce the engagement's off six months from now.'

'That's not going to work for me,' Brandon replied, knowing it was God's honest truth. He *wanted* this marriage, and not just for all the perfectly valid reasons he had stated.

The desire to have Lacey where he wanted her— in his home, as his wife—was about more than just payback. It was also about more than his ferocious determination to protect his daughter from the things he had suffered when his mother had abandoned him to a man who had paraded him in front of the world's media as his heir…

And it didn't have much at all to do with his desire to safeguard the Atlanta deal. It wasn't even solely down to the fierce need which pulsed through his veins every time he got within ten feet of this woman. A need he had never experienced with any other woman. But he'd be damned if he'd acknowledge any of those wayward emotions in front of Lacey. Because it would give her too much power, and she already had more power over him than he had ever allowed any woman.

'Why not?' Lacey asked, her eyes wide with confusion now.

His temper snapped. 'Because she is my child and I want full parental rights,' he said. Marrow had outlined earlier that marriage, as well as establishing paternity, would be the best way for him to gain full parental rights for his child. Surely that fact was more than enough to explain his sudden fierce determination to marry Lacey Carstairs…? 'So you'll never be able to stop me from having a relationship with her again.'

She flinched. 'But you can still have a relationship with Ruby—'

'Not good enough,' he cut her off. 'Why should I trust you to keep up your end of that bargain?'

'Because I'm her mother…' she began. 'And I want what's best for her. I know I made a mistake not telling you about her, but—'

'So what if you're her mother? That guarantees nothing,' he cut in again, the bitter laugh disguising the hollow pain in his chest. He hated her in that moment, for bringing that old vulnerability back. The flash of anger—and agony—was so intense, he blurted out the truth. 'My own mother sold me to my father when I was three months old as part of her ten-million-pound divorce settlement. And then she turned up again when I was seventeen, after he died, to ask for more money. Because apparently she'd spent it all,' he snarled. 'A mother's desire to do the right thing for her child can be bartered to the highest bidder, just like everything else.'

'But that's…hideous.' The utter shock on Lacey's face had him realising he'd said too much.

Far too much.

What the hell was wrong with him? He'd exposed himself. Had told her something he'd never revealed to anyone, other than a few of his employees—who were legally bound to keep his secrets. Unlike Lacey.

'I'm…so sorry,' she continued, the compassion darkening her eyes only making him feel more exposed, and more angry—with himself now, as much as her. 'Your mother sounds like no kind of mother at all.'

He sucked in a staggered breath and yanked himself viciously back from the edge.

Damn it, he didn't need or want her sympathy. Nor did he need her understanding. Why had he even bothered to explain himself? He didn't even owe her that much.

'Don't worry, I got over it a long time ago,' he said, burying the old trauma deep again so he could forget about it. His mother had no power to hurt him any more and she hadn't for a long time.

He had exorcised Elise Cade from his life when she had turned up unexpectedly at the reading of his father's will. He'd seen through her simpering regrets and her desire to 'form a relationship' with him almost instantly… But he was still furious that, for one giddy, idiotic moment, he had believed she might genuinely care for him. He could still feel that sudden leap in his heartrate when she'd introduced herself—and thrown her arms around his neck—the resentment he should have felt momentarily blindsided by that idiotic spurt of hope, of emotion.

Of course, she'd jettisoned her maternal act as soon as he'd tested her, and had been all too eager to grasp the large sum of money he'd offered her to leave him alone and never contact him again. But it had taken considerably longer to destroy that hollow pain all over again—that feeling of inadequacy, of desperation, which had haunted him as a child. And made him want things he shouldn't need.

He stared at Lacey now, wishing he could take the stupid revelation back, especially when she spoke again.

'I can't marry you, Brandon, just because you don't trust me. I understand why you don't trust me. But you have to believe me when I tell you I'm willing to do everything in my power to help you form a relationship with your daughter, and make up for the terrible mistake I made not telling you about her existence much, much sooner.'

Yeah, right.

He could hear the regret in her voice, and the guilt. But he could also hear that damn compassion. Maybe she really believed what she was telling him. But it wasn't enough. He refused to be at her mercy, or anyone else's, when it came to claiming his child. Marriage was the only thing that would give him the power he needed, not just as Ruby's father, but also to explore whatever the heck it was about this woman that he couldn't seem to exorcise no matter how hard he tried. But he could see from the intransigent look on her face she was determined not to budge. And he'd be damned if he'd risk exposing any more of his past to persuade her otherwise.

'I'll have my driver take you home,' he said, vindicated by the stunned surprise which suffused her features. 'I'll contact you to arrange a meeting with my daughter.'

'Okay,' she said, her relief palpable.

But, as she rushed out of the office, his gaze tracked her the whole way.

She'd expected him to put up more of a fight. But there was really no need, he thought, as the turmoil of emotions finally released their stranglehold on him enough to allow him to think coherently.

The story would break tomorrow, forcing Lacey to realise exactly how untenable her position—and the position she was putting their child in—really was.

And, when she finally came to her senses and accepted the inevitable—that she needed this marriage—he would be waiting.

CHAPTER NINE

'I CAN'T EVEN contact Ruby's nursery to say she can't come in today,' Lacey murmured as she peeked through the blind to stare at the press horde which had been massing outside their front door since before dawn. The crowd of photographers and reporters was now four rows deep, covering the pavement and most of the road.

She dropped the blind as one of the photographers spotted her and the barrage of shouted questions—which they had been attempting to ignore for two hours now—began again.

'Lacey, tell us about you and Cade.'

'Where's your daughter, Lacey, is she okay?'

'Are you going to sue him?'

Her stomach twisted, but the anxious knots in her gut were nothing compared to the guilt as she turned to see Milly, a concerned expression on her face, holding a sleepy Ruby—who had been woken by all the commotion.

'Mummy, why are they shouting?' Ruby said, rubbing her eyes.

Lacey crossed the room to lift her daughter into her arms. 'It's okay, baby. They'll get bored soon and go away.'

Although she didn't hold out much hope of that happening. They couldn't leave the flat, couldn't even turn on their phones, because both she and Milly had been inundated with calls and texts. How had they got her number and her address so easily?

She'd called the police an hour ago, but they'd said there was nothing they could do as long as the photographers and reporters remained off the premises.

And she was pretty sure she was now effectively out of a job. Melody had rung ten minutes ago—ostensibly to ask what was happening with the piece on Brandon. But she'd heard the wheedling tone in Melody's voice. Her editor knew about Ruby's relationship to him now, just like the rest of the world—and she was hoping for an exclusive. When Lacey had told her she couldn't write the piece, Melody had not been happy. Lacey had no doubt at all she would sack her eventually, when she refused to budge—and she was probably already bad-mouthing her all over the industry.

She'd thought she'd be prepared for this, thought she could weather the media storm, but Brandon had been right—they couldn't weather this. Protecting Ruby was her main concern now. Why had she lost sight of that so easily yesterday, when Brandon had demanded marriage? She'd thought she had a choice, but how long could she subject her child to this?

'Perhaps we should call Brandon Cade?' Milly

supplied, having to raise her voice to be heard above the commotion outside. 'He's responsible for this disaster, after all,' she added.

Except he wasn't, Lacey thought, remembering the stark emotion on his face yesterday when he'd revealed the grim truth about his parents' divorce and his mother's mercenary behaviour.

She'd realised almost instantly he hadn't intended to tell her so much. Certainly, he hadn't wanted to elicit any sympathy. But it was there none the less, pounding under her breastbone, right alongside the panic and anxiety about Ruby's welfare—and the choices she might be forced to make now to keep her child safe.

Brandon had offered her a way out. And she hadn't taken it. She'd refused to even consider it. She hadn't even questioned him about the sort of marriage he was suggesting. Because, when he had offered marriage, a foolish part of her heart had wanted to read much more into the offer than had actually been there. And that had scared the hell out of her.

If she called him now, she would at least have to consider his solution. But how could she ensure she remained pragmatic about such an arrangement? Because she didn't feel pragmatic about anything any more, not after getting that crucial insight into the boy he'd once been, the lonely, manipulated child behind the man. His mask of power and entitlement had slipped, and as a result the girl she'd been—that fanciful, romantic, needy girl—had come back out of hiding.

And that was before she even factored in his clear commitment to becoming a father to Ruby. He wanted full parental rights, and how could she argue against that when she had kept his daughter's existence a secret from him for so long?

'Do you think he'd be willing to help us?' Milly asked, getting a little frantic.

Lacey nodded. 'Yes,' she said, knowing the answer to that much at least was fairly easy. He had told her he was determined to protect Ruby and she believed him.

She handed Ruby back to Milly and tugged her phone out of her pocket. But, before she had the chance to switch it back on, the commotion from outside became deafening.

She rushed to the window. 'What the…?'

A long black limousine had pulled up at the kerb, followed by two more cars. The army of press rushed the vehicles, the camera flashes and shouts reaching a crescendo of sound and fury. Several burly security guards leapt out of the cars behind the limo and proceeded to push the tidal wave back.

Then Brandon stepped out of the limousine, spoke to the driver, who also appeared, then took the steps to Lacey's front door in quick strides. He ignored the shouts and long lenses with a steely determination borne of familiarity, she suspected. Her own heart galloped into her throat, though. Relief was followed by a stupid feeling of euphoria.

He had come to rescue them, to rescue his daughter.

His gaze locked on her face—implacable, deter-

mined, but strangely devoid of judgment. She stared
back at him, frozen for a moment in the tractor beam
of those cool green eyes. Then he nodded at the front
door.

She scrambled off the sofa and rushed out of the
flat to open the front door.

He stepped inside, then slammed the door, shut-
ting out the paparazzi and the barrage of noise behind him.

'Thank you for coming,' she said, feeling giddy
with relief and something that felt disturbingly like
exhilaration. Why should she be so happy to see
him? When everything about this situation was a
disaster?

The anxious knots in her stomach tightened. He
had made what he wanted clear yesterday, and he
would not give up on his goal.

Reaction streaked through her—visceral and volatile and yet somehow helping to stop her knees from
dissolving—when he cupped her elbow and led her
back down the corridor.

'You have five minutes to pack what you need.
You and Ruby are relocating to the Cade estate in
Wiltshire. You'll be safe there until this dies down. I
have a secure apartment Milly can stay in near here
if she doesn't wish to join you there.'

She could have objected. He wasn't giving her a
choice. And it would mean resigning her job. But,
given her editor was likely to fire her soon anyway,
and with the feeding frenzy outside still audible, did
she really *have* a choice? As they re-entered the liv-

ing room, and she saw Ruby's head cradled on Milly's shoulder—her little girl trying to hide from the scary noise—the decision was made for her.

She would accept Brandon's offer of a safe place to stay, and deal with any strings he might attach to it later.

'About time you showed up,' Milly said, rushing towards them both. 'I'll take the flat, thanks. I've got to get to work.' she added, clearly having heard the conversation in the hallway. 'Here.' Lifting Ruby, she handed her towards Brandon. 'Ruby, Mummy's friend Brandon is going to hold you while Mummy and me pack some stuff to take with us. Then we can get away from the annoying people outside, okay baby?' Milly coaxed when Ruby continued to cling to her.

Lacey felt Brandon tense beside her. Her heart bounced painfully in her chest, knowing how big a deal this was for him. From the frown creasing his forehead, she suspected he had never held a child before now. But when Lacey stepped forward, intending to defuse the moment and take Ruby instead, her little girl lifted her arms towards Brandon—trusting him instinctively.

A sharp frown furrowed his brow, but he hesitated for less than a second before scooping Ruby into his arms.

'I don't like the shouting, Mr Brandon,' Ruby said, before shoving her thumb into her mouth and wrapping her other arm around his neck. She buried her head against his broad chest as Milly raced out of the room.

Lacey's heart swelled painfully as Brandon placed a comforting hand on his child's back and murmured, 'Don't worry. I'm going to take you away from the shouting.'

His gaze lifted to Lacey, who still stood rooted to the spot, trapped by the emotions charging through her body at the devastating sight of her daughter, *their* daughter, held so securely in his arms.

What she saw in his face—guarded tension, but also grim determination and fierce protectiveness—had the guilt all but crippling her. She had denied them both so much. How could she ever make amends?

But then she was jolted out of her revelry by his husky command. 'Stop standing there and start packing, Lacey. You have exactly four minutes left now.'

Thirteen hours later, Lacey stood on the steps of the lavish sixty-room Palladian mansion she had arrived at that morning, the manicured gardens now dark as night fell. A sense of unreality settled over her—which had been chasing her all day—as she watched the Cade Inc helicopter appear and settle on the side lawn, not far from the covered swimming pool where she and Ruby had been swimming that afternoon.

Nerves tangled and tightened in her stomach.

They hadn't spoken since Brandon's driver had dropped Brandon at Cade Tower that morning, before the limousine had headed towards Wiltshire and the Cade estate. And, during the brief time they had been together, she had spent most of it calming Ruby down after their scary dash through the herd of photographers and reporters—only barely held back by Brandon's security guards.

The chopper's noise wasn't muffled much by the nearby forest but she doubted even an earthquake would have woken Ruby, who had gone to sleep hours ago in the suite which had been prepared for them—complete with a slew of new toys for Ruby—in the house's east wing.

It had been an exhausting day—not least because Lacey's mind had replayed the parting words Brandon had whispered to her as Ruby slept in her car seat for the last thirteen hours straight.

'Marriage is the only way to solve this situation, Lacey. Next time I see you, we are going to have that conversation again.'

Lacey clasped her arms around her waist to control the speedy thumps of her heartbeat as Brandon emerged from the chopper flanked by Daryl and another assistant she didn't recognise. He strode towards her, his dark suit pressed against his tall physique in the downdraft from the blades.

She'd received a text from Daryl two hours ago, informing her Brandon would be arriving late and that he would speak to her in the morning. But she had decided not to wait. Sleep would be impossible with 'that conversation' hanging over her head. Plus, she needed to thank him properly for coming to her family's rescue that morning—and for letting her sister stay rent-free in a lavish gated condo in Islington which Milly had rung her to rave about that afternoon.

The anxiety that had been kept ruthlessly at bay all day squeezed Lacey's ribs as he approached.

What exactly was she going to do about his offer of marriage? Because yesterday's certainty that a marriage between them would be a disaster felt a lot less certain now.

He reached her at last, his eyes dark in the twilight. 'Hello, Lacey,' he said, his voice gruff. 'I told Daryl to tell you I would be late,' he added, the frown suggesting he wasn't *that* pleased to see her.

She tried not to take his abrupt manner personally. He had to be tired too. She knew he had been dealing with the fallout from the Drystar headlines all day. He'd even been forced to hold an impromptu press conference which she knew he must have hated. He was a man who guarded his privacy, and now she knew why. This morning had been a terrifying wake-up call. But, while she and Ruby had been whisked away to safety, Brandon had stayed to face the fallout alone.

'I know,' she said, and shivered, the nerves doing strange things to her insides. 'I wanted to stay up to thank you. And to…to discuss what you said earlier.'

Daryl and the other assistant bade them both goodbye and headed towards the staff cottages on the other side of the gardens. Brandon nodded at the doorman, who was waiting to lock the main door behind them.

'Let's get a drink,' he said abruptly, and touched her elbow to lead her into an imposing library situated off the main entrance hall.

The graze of his fingertips was electrifying in the quiet country night as the sound of the chopper blades outside finally died.

He crossed the silk rug to a drinks cabinet in the far wall. The scent of old leather and lemon polish filled the musty air. He switched on a small light that cast a soft glow over his harsh features.

He wasn't just tired, she realised. He was exhausted. The bruised smudges under his eyes made him look more unsettled—and somehow more vulnerable—than she had ever seen him.

Without asking, he poured them both a whisky and handed her a glass. 'Here.'

She took the crystal tumbler, shivering again when his fingers brushed hers.

He stepped back, watching her intently over the rim of the glass as he knocked the whisky back in one gulp.

'So, what exactly did you wish to thank me for?' he asked, breaking eye contact at last to pour himself another glass.

'For arriving this morning, and then protecting me and Ruby and Milly from what you had to go through today,' she said simply.

'She's my daughter. What did you think I would do?' he replied sharply. 'Leave the three of you to be picked apart by those vultures?'

She heard the bitterness in his tone, and the accusation, and the guilt she had been determined to suppress leapt from the shadows to torment her again. 'I'm sorry, I underestimated you.'

'Yes, you did,' he said, still studying her. Her heart started to make her gag, and she realised how close she was to tears.

Clearly, she was tired and emotional too, because maintaining the fragile truce between them suddenly seemed so important. It probably wouldn't last. But, now more than ever, she was determined to figure out a solution that they could both live with.

'I still want marriage, Lacey,' he said before she had the chance to say more.

Her breath hitched in her lungs at the determination in his voice. She thought she'd been prepared to deal with this conversation now… Apparently not.

She took a sip of the peaty whisky, the burn of the liquor as she swallowed masking the painful burn already there before she replied. 'I know you don't trust me to let you form a relationship without…'

He held up his hand and she stuttered to a halt.

'It's not just that,' he said, the strain lines around his mouth relaxing a little. 'You need my protection, Lacey. Both you and Ruby. Surely today's experience proved that conclusively? I can't give you that protection unless I claim her unequivocally as mine. And that means marriage.'

She stared down at the amber liquid in her glass. She could argue that they didn't have to be wed for him to claim Ruby. Or that Ruby was a child, not a piece of property who he needed to own. But the protests dried up inside her at the visceral memory of the way he'd held his child for the first time, and the sight of him charging through the crowd of reporters while Ruby had clung to him, trusting him completely, as they made their way to the car.

Ruby needed her father. How could she continue to deny that after this morning?

But, as she tried to figure out how best to proceed, he continued, his tone brittle but no less forceful.

'This isn't just about Ruby, though. It's also about us,' he said.

Us.

The word seemed to reverberate in her chest—part promise, part threat—as her head jerked up.

'What about us?' she managed, forcing herself not to relinquish eye contact. Whatever happened now, she would not let the fanciful girl she'd once been misconstrue his intentions again.

'I'm going to need your help getting to know Ruby,' he said. 'A *lot* of your help. Because, believe me, fatherhood is not something that is likely to come naturally to me,' he added.

The dark tide of sympathy pulsed in her chest. His uncertainty was surprising but also deeply touching…and illuminating.

He was struggling as well with the enormity of this situation—why hadn't she considered he might not be as confident as he appeared? It also seemed important that he'd let her glimpse his vulnerability. Because she suspected showing a weakness was something he despised.

'Marriage is the best way for us to get to know each other properly,' he added. 'I want Ruby to trust me. And, for her to trust me, I need to trust you. We need to spend time together for that to happen.'

She took another sip of the whisky. 'Okay,' she said.

Something fierce and visceral flared in his gaze. 'Okay, you'll marry me?'

'Okay, I'll consider it,' she replied.

Brandon let out a strained laugh. He'd been considering this conversation all day. He'd been prepared to bully and cajole her if necessary into doing what he thought was best. But, as usual, Lacey had blindsided him. Almost as much as the experience of holding his daughter in his arms for the first time had blindsided him that morning.

Seeing his child and Lacey and her sister trapped in their home by those bastards, feeling his little girl cling to him and rely on him for her safety, had changed something fundamental inside him. Until that moment, the concept of becoming a father had seemed purely academic in a lot of ways.

Now it felt very real.

'What exactly is there to consider?' he said, deciding to humour her. After all, they'd both had a long, tiring day. And she seemed a lot more malleable than she had yesterday in his office. Perhaps it was time to employ the carrot instead of the stick—something he should have considered sooner. He prided himself on being a master of negotiation, but for some damn reason as soon as he got a lungful of Lacey's scent, and saw the bold pride in her eyes, he found it impossible to back off with her.

Perhaps because he wanted this marriage, so much.

Eventually he would get bored with her. He had no track record when it came to long-term commitment, nor did he desire one. At which point they could consider a divorce. Somehow he doubted his fascination with Lacey would wear off any time soon—after all, it had lasted five years already—but when it did, if he had established a workable relationship with his daughter, then it would be all good.

'Exactly what kind of marriage are you expecting?' she asked, her cheeks mottling with colour.

He frowned. 'The usual kind.' Why was she talking in riddles?

'So you don't plan for this to be a marriage in name only?'

He choked out an astonished laugh at her naivety—breaking the tension in his gut for the first time in close to a week. 'Of course not. Why would either one of us want a sexless marriage?'

He cupped her cheek, no longer able to resist the powerful urge to touch her. Did a little of that girl still remain? And why did the thought of discovering the answer to that question feel as hot as it was beguiling?

'Sex happens to be the only thing we do well together,' he said. 'Why deny ourselves that pleasure

when we're probably going to be fighting fires on
every other front in this marriage?'

Funny to think, though, that fighting those fires
with her appealed to him almost as much as the
thought of taking her in every possible way he could
imagine. And he'd imagined a lot.

She turned away, but he saw her throat contract
as she swallowed.

*That's right, Lacey, why deny it when you know
it's true?*

He let his hand drop, remembering that in any
negotiation it was sometimes better to stake your
claim then wait for your opponent to come to you.

'Of course, it will be your choice. I'm not going
to force the issue,' he added.

*Not when seducing you will be so much more re-
warding.*

At last she nodded, but something flickered in her
eyes that he couldn't read.

'I see,' she said. He had to bite his lip to stop himself from smiling again. She'd learn soon enough
that resistance was futile when it came to denying
their chemistry.

He tensed as her breath gushed out.

'Let me demonstrate,' he said, sliding a knuckle
under her chin.

What the hell was he waiting for? He wanted this
marriage, and he wanted her. But, more to the point,
she wanted him with the same intensity. It was high
time she admitted that.

Lifting her face to his, he slanted his lips across hers.

She opened for him instinctively, proving his point perfectly, but then the need and hunger overwhelmed him with startling speed.

She tasted of whisky and sweetness as his tongue tangled with hers—demanding, dominant, all-consuming. She kissed him back with passion and purpose, all the stress, the volatile emotions of the last few days, swept away on a furious wave of desire.

Her hands flattened on his stomach as he gripped her head, angling her mouth to take more. To take all. His abs trembled as her fingers fisted in the starched cotton to draw him closer.

He broke the kiss reluctantly, but he could see she had got the point when he searched her face—flushed and glowing in the muted light—and saw his own need reflected back at him.

'Marry me, Lacey,' he said, his voice husky.

She stepped back, her teeth chewing on her bottom lip. He waited, her answer suddenly meaning much more than he wanted it to.

She nodded, even as the wary tension remained.

'All right, I'll marry you,' she said. The spurt of triumph was swiftly quashed, though, when she added, 'But I would like separate bedrooms.'

No way.

He pursed his lips to stop the swift, knee-jerk response from shooting out of his mouth.

What was the matter with him? He never shared a bedroom—why would he wish to share one with her?

'If that's what you want.' He pushed the irrational anger down and forced an assured smile to his lips.

'I don't see that being a deal-breaker. But I want to arrange the wedding as soon as possible.' He wasn't going to allow her time to change her mind.

'Okay,' she said. As she turned and walked away from him, the triumph surged back.

After all, her request did not preclude him from exploiting their volatile chemistry as soon as they were wed.

CHAPTER TEN

THE NEXT MORNING, Brandon strode towards the mansion's east wing, feeling drained and out of sorts—emotions he did not want to feel already playing havoc with his usual purpose.

Predictably, he'd had a virtually sleepless night—*again*—thanks mostly to their drive-by kiss last night in the library. And the realisation that, while Lacey had agreed to marriage, she still had the power to unsettle him far too much.

But then, he had been exhausted yesterday. It had been a horrendous day. He hated talking to the press at the best of times. And having to return to a house that held so many bad memories hadn't improved his disposition either.

He passed the door to his father's study and kept walking. But, even so, the familiar chill slithered down his spine, much as it had when he'd been a boy.

The news had never been good when he had been called to the austere room. His father had always had complaints, demands, criticisms and a host of other ways to show him how he was falling short as the heir to the Cade empire. Even now he couldn't remember a single word of praise or affection.

He rarely stayed at the estate unless he had to, because being here reminded him of that insecure, far too obedient child who had taken all the constant criticism and internalised them far too readily.

His footsteps echoed on the polished parquet flooring as he forced himself to forget that boy. At last, he reached the far end of the corridor that led to the rooms Lacey and Ruby had moved into the previous day.

He stopped outside the door to their suite and detected the muffled sounds of a child's laughter. His heartbeat accelerated, the familiar anxiety from so long ago clawing at his throat.

Don't be an idiot, Cade. She's a four-year-old child. And you couldn't possibly be as much of a bastard as he was—even if you wanted to be, which you don't.

The marriage Lacey had agreed to last night would smooth the way to forming a relationship with his child. Plus, the head groundskeeper had given him an idea about what to do with his daughter today. Even so, his arm felt as if it weighed several tons as he lifted it and rapped three times on the door.

The laughter cut off and the door swung open.

Lacey stood in front of him wearing a pair of yoga pants which accentuated her slender curves and a flimsy camisole top which clung to her breasts. With her feet bare, her face devoid of make-up and her short cap of curls rioting around her face, she looked as if she'd only just got out of bed.

Heat shot straight into his groin on cue. Heat and something far more volatile—which felt annoyingly like yearning.

Damn.

Why couldn't his feelings be as simple and straightforward as they should be where this woman was concerned?

'Brandon?' she whispered. 'Hi. We weren't expecting you.'

He frowned, realising maybe he should have mentioned his planned visit to prepare the child for his arrival. Then he inwardly cursed himself. This was precisely why he was nervous. He had no clue what he was doing.

But, before he could figure out what to say, she swung the door wider to welcome him into the room.

'Why don't you join Ruby and I for breakfast?' she said, the smile on her lips somewhat contradicted by the mottled flush on her collar bone, visible where the worn camisole drooped.

'Okay, sure,' he said, but then wondered how Lacey would introduce him. He didn't want her to break the news to Ruby that he was her father yet. It was too soon—she needed to get to know him first. The last thing he wished to do was frighten her, the way his own father had so often frightened him.

Perhaps you should have mentioned all that to her last night, before kissing her senseless.

But, as he stepped into the room, Lacey solved the

problem. 'Ruby, you remember Brandon?' she said. 'He carried you to the car yesterday. He's going to have breakfast with us.'

A little of his panic retreated until he spotted the child—his daughter—dressed in pyjamas decorated with multi-coloured dinosaurs, sitting at the breakfast table in the far corner of the room. And the same thought he had had yesterday when she'd clung to him so readily blindsided him again.

She's so small. How can she be so perfect and yet so tiny?

He cleared his throat as he stood suspended in the room. 'Hello, Ruby,' he managed.

She looked at him inquisitively. 'Hello, Mr Brandon,' she said.

The 'Mr' made him wince, reminding him of his father, who had always insisted he call him 'sir'. 'You can call me Brandon,' he said. 'If you prefer.'

'Okay,' she said, looking nonplussed. He knew how she felt. Could this get any more awkward? How on earth did you talk to a four-year-old?

But then he recalled what his groundskeeper had mentioned that morning when he'd gone for his morning run. He knew nothing about children, but he remembered what it was like to be a child himself. And he wasn't above bribing his way into his daughter's affection if need be.

'I thought we could go to the groundskeeper's cottage this morning. His dog, Maisey, had some puppies two months ago and they are looking for homes for them.' He glanced at Lacey, who was watching him with a soft light in her eyes, which would have been unsettling if he hadn't already gone right past awkward to extremely uncomfortable. 'If your mother agrees, I thought perhaps you might like one,' he added.

'A puppy!' The little girl gasped, her whole face lighting up as if stars had exploded behind her eyes. 'Really? Can I have a puppy, Mummy? Can I?' she asked Lacey, her small voice rising and her whole body bouncing with so much excitement, Brandon became momentarily concerned she might actually burst.

'Yes, of course, I think that would be a wonderful idea,' Lacey said.

Before she finished talking, the little girl leapt off her chair and shot towards Brandon as if she had been fired from a gun.

He barely had a chance to brace before she barrelled into him and wrapped chubby arms around his knees.

She tipped her head back to beam at him. 'Thank you, thank you, thank you, Mr Brandon,' she said, having forgotten his suggestion about dropping the Mr already. But somehow it didn't seem to matter, as her green eyes sparkled with happiness, the dimple in her cheek winking at him in delight.

He stared down at her, with absolutely no idea what to say or do, his heart hitting his chest wall in painful thuds, the protective instinct wrapping round his heart like a lasso at the thought of how vulnerable she was, how innocent and guileless.

Could it really be this easy to win her trust?

'Can we go now? Can we, please?' she asked.

It occurred to him how much he had to learn as he opened his mouth to say yes—ready to give her whatever she wanted—but Lacey interrupted them gently.

'We need to finish our breakfast first, Rubes. And then you need to get dressed. You can't pick a puppy in your pyjamas, now, can you?'

The child giggled, still delighted. 'No, I can't. I don't want my puppy to think I'm silly.'

Instead of being intimidated, or even phased by his obvious inexperience with children, she let go of his legs and held her small hand up to him. He took it instinctively. As her soft fingers tightened on his, miraculously the clawing panic began to loosen its grip on his throat.

'If it's a girl puppy, I'm going to call her Tinker-bell,' she said as she tugged him towards the breakfast table.

She continued to chatter at a staggering rate as Lacey served him breakfast. Luckily, his daughter didn't seem to require any input from him—which was good, because he was actually speechless.

For the first time ever, though, he found himself more than happy simply to go with the flow.

Lacey eased the door shut to Ruby's room, where her daughter had finally collapsed for a well-earned nap—after spending the morning with her father and her new Jack Russell puppy, Tinkerbell—and sent a careful smile to the man beside her…who was frowning as he stared at the door.

'She's exhausting,' he murmured.

Brandon Cade looked shell-shocked—but somehow the perplexed expression as he turned that fierce green gaze on her only made her heart swell more.

He'd been so patient with Ruby today—thoughtful, attentive and utterly fascinated by everything Ruby did or said. He'd also seemed more than a little nervous, which was a new look for him. Lacey had sensed as soon as he had walked into their room four hours ago—and Ruby had treated him to one of her 'special hugs'—he was completely and utterly out of his depth.

The puppy suggestion, though, had been nothing short of inspired. And she couldn't help wondering where it had come from… Because, for a man who had told her he didn't think he would be a natural at fatherhood, he had already found a direct route into his little girl's heart.

'She's excited,' Lacey clarified.

He nodded. 'She really adores that puppy,' he said. 'I never knew someone could be so erudite and articulate on a single topic for four solid hours.'

Lacey chuckled, the warmth in her chest glowing. It felt good to be able to talk about her child with him. *Their* child. Who knew?

'Yes, she already loves Tinkerbell,' she replied. 'She also likes you rather a lot.'

A flicker of surprise crossed his features. 'I'm glad,' he said, sinking a hand into his pocket. 'I just…' He hesitated. 'I don't want her to be frightened of me.'

'She isn't,' Lacey replied, puzzled.

Why would Ruby be frightened of him when he had been so careful with her today? He'd answered all of her questions and listened intently to the endless stream of information on her new puppy. He'd even carried her back from the groundsman's cottage after she'd begun to tire, holding Ruby securely as she dropped off to sleep with surprising confidence, given Lacey was sure it was only the second time he had held a child in his life.

'I'm sure the puppy didn't hurt,' he added wryly.

'Tinkerbell's not the only reason,' she said, determined to reassure him and knowing it was true. 'What made you suggest the puppy?' she asked, intrigued.

'I've never been above using bribery when it comes to getting what I want,' he said, his voice deepening as his gaze met hers. Even as a familiar reaction pulsed in her abdomen, she could hear the evasive tone. Was he trying to distract her?

'True,' she said, the provocative comment reminding her of last night's kiss, as she was sure it had been intended to do. 'But a puppy was a brilliant idea. I just wondered if there was a reason you thought of it,' she probed again, determined not to be distracted.

He shrugged, but the movement was tense. He didn't answer straight away. Instead, his gaze slid away from hers to contemplate the view, from the

room's huge paned window, of the mansion's manicured lawns now drenched in sunshine.

Instinctively she knew there'd been more to the
idea now. And that he was trying to decide whether
to confide in her or not.

Her chest tightened as she realised how much she
wanted to know the truth, because it might give her
another crucial insight into his childhood.

At last, his gaze met hers, direct, unflinching, but
filled with a depth of emotion she suspected he had
not intended her to see.

'Tinkerbell is the descendant of a puppy I once
owned when I was a child here,' he said. Something
flashed in his gaze that looked bitter and angry, but
beneath it she could see the shadow of hurt.

His voice, though, remained flat and hollow when
he continued. 'I adored that little Jack Russell. He
was my best friend. My *only* friend, really,' he said,
then let out a humourless laugh. 'I was brought up
alone by the staff here ever since I was a baby. I
didn't see my father often, but on one of his rare vis-
its he must have spotted me playing with my puppy.
The head groundsman—John's father,' he added,
mentioning the man they had met that day. 'Had
given him to me for my fifth birthday two months
before. When I was called into my father's study, I
was excited. I had some childish notion he was going
to give me a birthday present, even though he'd never
given me one before. Instead, he told me it was high
time I went to boarding school and that the puppy

would be taken from me and rehoused—because the staff couldn't look after it while I was gone.'

Lacey gasped. 'But…how could he do something so cruel?' she said, shocked not just by his father's cruelty, and the decision to send his son away to boarding school at such a young age, but also by the lack of emotion in Brandon's voice.

He shrugged, as if the incident was of no importance, the expression on his face blank. 'He wanted to toughen me up, he said.'

'Your father sounds like an ass,' she said forcefully, suddenly furious with the man. Was this why Brandon controlled his emotions so carefully?

'He was.' He stared at her, a muscle twitching in his jaw. 'But, to be fair to him, it worked.'

'Did it?' she asked, the compassion welling in her chest.

Unlike when her father had rejected her and Milly, Brandon had had no one, and that sickened her.

She cradled his cheek, felt it harden beneath her palm.

'Don't…' He tugged away from her touch. 'Don't mistake me for that lonely boy, Lacey.'

She lowered her hand, seeing the shutters she had managed to pry open—at least a little bit—slam back down.

'I'm not that pathetic, defenceless child any more,' he added. 'These days, I consider solitude my strength.'

It was a warning. She got that. A warning not to

assume that any kindness, any affection he showed towards his daughter, would be extended to her.

But, even so, she couldn't help imagining that small boy, treated with such callous indifference by the man who should have nurtured him.

And the man that boy had become, who had worked so hard today to form a bond with his own child, a child he hadn't even known existed a week ago.

Maybe he didn't want Lacey's compassion. But he had it regardless—along with her admiration.

Plus, she had never considered solitude a strength, and she was damned if she was going to start now.

'Have you spoken to Ruby yet about the wedding?' he asked.

'Um…no, not yet,' she said, disconcerted by the change of subject, but willing to go with it. She needed time to get all the emotions making her chest ache under control so she could face him again tomorrow with her armour intact.

'I thought…' She paused. 'I thought maybe we could tell her together?'

His brow furrowed. 'I'm afraid that won't be possible, not unless you want to wait for at least a fortnight. I'm heading to the States this afternoon—the Atlanta deal fell through, so I'm going to scope out alternative options. I probably won't be back until the wedding.'

'Oh.' Lacey's heart sank. Despite the constant tension between them, she realised she would miss him.

Seeing him with his daughter, finding out more

about his childhood, had given her a compelling insight into the man behind the mask of power and control he wore for the world.

He didn't want her to know that man—he had made that clear. But she had agreed to marry him in three weeks' time—which meant she needed to find out much more about him, whether he wanted her to or not.

'By the way, the PR team have suggested we consider a honeymoon after the wedding. A week at Cade Island in Bermuda should be enough to convince the media this is a real marriage.' His gaze focussed on her face, making the skin on her neck and chin, sensitive from last night's voracious kiss, prickle. 'We can take Ruby with us, if you would like?'

He was offering her a way out, a chance to use their child as a go-between. And, while on one level she suspected the offer was a genuine one, the look in his eyes suggested this was also a challenge, to see if she would take the coward's way out.

If they went on this honeymoon alone, there would be no avoiding the chemistry that had exploded last night without warning. But why should that be a bad thing? Surely a week in paradise would give her the opportunity she needed to find out if this could really be a real marriage?

She took a deep breath, let it out slowly.

Go for it, Lacey. It's worth the risk.

She shook her head. 'Ruby's had too much disruption to her routine already. Plus, she'd never want to leave Tinkerbell for that length of time. And Milly will be here to look after her.'

Her sister was arriving at the end of the week, as the school where she worked had been besieged by the press too, and the decision had been made for her to join them in Wiltshire for a week or so.

Heat flared in his eyes. 'Okay, I'll make the travel arrangements for the two of us.' He checked his watch. 'I need to leave.' He glanced back towards the bedroom where Ruby slept. 'Say goodbye to Ruby for me. I guess we can tell her about the wedding arrangements together on a video link?' he offered.

The intuitive suggestion made her realise that, while Brandon had been out of his depth first thing that morning, he was already growing in confidence as Ruby's father.

Why did that not surprise her?

'Okay, I think that would work,' she said.

As he turned to go, an empty space opened up in her stomach at the thought of not seeing him again, in person, for weeks. But then he stopped and turned back.

'FYI, Lacey,' he said, his gaze blazing with that devastating combination of heat and purpose. 'You should organise a more reliable form of birth control than condoms before the honeymoon.'

Without another word, he walked out—leaving her hormones *and* her emotions in tatters.

Blast the man.

CHAPTER ELEVEN

Three weeks later

'RUBY, IT'S TIME to sleep now,' Lacey said as she eased her daughter's arms from around her neck.

'But I'm too happy, Mummy.' Ruby gave a huge yawn and settled back into her bed. 'Tinkerbell was such a good bridesmaid. She didn't even pee on your dress,' she added with a tired giggle. 'Isn't that true, Mr Brandon?' She sent Brandon, who stood behind Lacey, a sleepy grin.

They'd barely had a chance to talk since exchanging their vows five hours ago. Lacey in the designer concoction of lace and silk, with Brandon and her young daughter and the mischievous puppy—who Ruby had insisted on including in the ceremony— sandwiched between them as five hundred carefully selected guests had laughed and then applauded.

The lavish event seemed to have gone by in a blur of nerves and adrenaline, but Lacey's first sight of Brandon—in the perfectly tailored wedding suit, his green eyes gleaming—had sent her senses into over-drive, and they hadn't really touched the ground since.

She was exhausted now. And saying goodbye to her daughter was only making her more emotional. What had she done, marrying this man she barely knew? Every aspect of her life in Brandon's world seemed overwhelming, except the one thing that drew them together… Ruby.

So why had she agreed to leave her little girl behind tonight?

'Tinkerbell was a good bridesmaid,' Brandon said, resting a heavy hand on Lacey's shoulder, no doubt to present a loving front to their daughter. 'But not as good as you were, Ruby. I was so proud of you today.'

It was of course exactly the right thing to say, making Ruby's eyes brighten and her tired smile beam.

But then Ruby's smile faltered and her eyes filled with a longing Lacey didn't understand.

'Are you my daddy now?' she asked.

Brandon's hand tensed on her shoulder as Lacey's heart leapt into her throat at Ruby's innocent question. Brandon had video-called Ruby and her a number of times in the past three weeks while he'd been in the US—but, once they'd spoken to their daughter about the wedding, he had chosen not to broach the subject of his true identity.

Lacey had decided not to push. It was Brandon's decision when he told his daughter he was her father and she needed to respect that. But, even so, she could hear the thickening in his voice he couldn't disguise as he spoke.

'Yes, Ruby, I am your daddy,' he said. 'If you would like, you can call me Daddy instead of Mr Brandon.'

'Can I really?' Ruby asked, the innocent request made Lacey's heart break a little.

'Yes, I'd like you to,' he replied. 'Very much.'

A sleepy grin spread across Ruby's features. 'Latisha said it's sad I don't have a daddy,' she said, mentioning one of her little friends whose family they had invited to the event. 'But now I do.'

Guilt tightened Lacey's throat. Ruby had never mentioned not having a father to her before.

Leaning past her, Brandon planted a kiss on Ruby's forehead then pulled back, his expression for once unguarded, his eyes warm with affection. 'Your daddy says it's time to go to sleep.'

Ruby nodded. 'Okay, Daddy,' she said, clearly wanting to use the word as often as possible.

Lacey smiled, forcing the guilt back down as she tucked Ruby into the bed and kissed her too. 'Daddy and I will video-call you from the island every day over the next week. And Milly will be here to look after you, okay, Rubes?'

Ruby nodded again and did another jaw-breaking yawn. 'Milly says we can play with Tinkerbell tomorrow,' she said, sounding excited about the prospect. 'Night-night, Mummy and Daddy,' she added, then promptly turned over and dropped into a deep sleep, no doubt full of dreams of mischievous puppies and new daddies.

Lacey's heartbeat hammered in her throat as she stood, to find Brandon staring at her.

With his tie and jacket gone, the first few buttons of his white dress shirt undone and the shadow of new stubble covering his jaw, he looked rugged, relaxed and impossibly handsome. The fierce glow in his eyes didn't look remotely relaxed, though.

There were so many things she wanted to say to him—starting with apologising again for robbing him of the first four years of his child's life—but before she could unstick a single word he cut through the silence.

'You have twenty minutes to get changed and say your goodbyes, then I'll meet you at the heliport,' he said, his tone forceful and oddly detached, even as his gaze raked over her with deliberate intent.

As the heated look burned through the layers of silk and lace, and her nerves began to jump and jive, Lacey could sense the barriers he had let down during the day for the sake of the press, their friends and their child being put firmly back in place. Again.

She forced herself not to let her usual fear of rejection overwhelm her, though. Brandon Cade wasn't like her father. Maybe he didn't trust her yet. But, after seeing him with Ruby today, after feeling his eyes on her throughout the ceremony and reception, she was not about to give up hope.

She'd made a mistake five years ago. But she couldn't keep apologising for it for ever. This honeymoon would give them a chance to move past it. And she was determined not to squander the opportunity.

Brandon stood at the steps of the helicopter twenty minutes later and watched his new wife walk across the dark lawn towards him—the emotions he'd kept on a tight leash for five unending hours beginning to break their bounds. Wearing jeans, a T-shirt and a long jacket to guard against the evening's spring chill, she looked no less stunning than she had that morning when he'd turned to see her heading down the aisle of the small chapel on the mansion's grounds. Her sister and his daughter had been following behind her in matching gowns, the crowd enchanted by the antics of the little girl and the puppy she was trying to control on its leash, while his heart had jumped into his throat and remained there most of the day.

But all his attention was now focussed on the woman. She had her sister Milly by her side again, still dressed in her maid-of-honour gown.

The two women embraced and Milly sent him a wave.

He waved back before Milly turned to go back into the house, where the reception banquet had given way to a dance set by a famous DJ several hours ago.

Putting her head down, Lacey picked her way across the grass towards him, gripping the small backpack she had slung over her shoulder. The rest

of her honeymoon luggage had been loaded on the
chopper ten minutes ago.

He'd felt her nerves all through the day—from
the moment he'd lifted her veil and seen the sheen
of emotion and determination in her eyes.

However much of a formality this marriage was
supposed to be, to give Ruby the full protection of
his name and his wealth, however much of a damage limitation exercise it was to shore up his repu-
tation after the media furore of the past three weeks
around the disclosure of his 'secret child', it now felt
startlingly real.

He couldn't give her his heart and, more to the
point, he didn't want to give her his heart, because
the need for love had once made him weak.

But as she made her way towards him, her steps
slowing, the wary tension in her body building, he
recalled the stunned emotion piercing his chest when
his daughter had called him Daddy for the first time.

Okay, maybe he did have a heart. The fierce pride
and protectiveness he felt for Ruby was surely something close to love—or as close to love as he was
ever likely to get?

But loving his child was very different from loving her mother. And he needed to remember that.
Because loving his child did not hold the risks that
came with loving Lacey. He steeled himself against
the emotion squeezing his ribs as Lacey reached him
and he welcomed the swift spurt of arousal.

This wasn't love, it was simply lust.

The chopper's blades accelerated as the pilot prepared for take-off, the engine noise whipping away any possibility of conversation.

But, as she stopped in front of him, he lifted her chin to take her lips in a harsh kiss, his tongue plundering her mouth. So what if this wasn't a love match? He wanted her to know she was his now, in every way that mattered.

Her palms flattened against his abdomen.

He tore his lips away, refusing to take the kiss deeper, determined to maintain control.

He'd waited for three weeks, the hunger building each time he'd seen her on the video link, going a little nuts when she had been beside him while they'd exchanged their vows and later as she'd sat next to him during the never-ending wedding banquet.

But there was something about seeing her with Ruby…with *his* child…that only made him want her more… And he wanted her too damn much already.

She'd played the part of the eager bride well during the day. But he knew the stunned desire in her gaze was entirely genuine. Good, because he planned to make her wait now, even if it killed him.

He refused to allow this fierce desire to put him at a disadvantage again.

Leading her into the chopper without a word, he watched her strap herself in with trembling fingers.

He was glad she had agreed to honeymoon with him alone. As much as he adored Ruby's company, adored getting to know all the fascinating facets of his child, he also needed to ensure he took the edge off his desire for her mother. He didn't want his physical needs to detract from what this marriage was meant to achieve.

His feelings for Lacey were far more complex than they should be. He'd already told her much more than he'd ever told any woman about his past, his miserable childhood. He couldn't afford to let Lacey get any closer or he could fall into the trap of wanting more from her. And that would give her a power over him he had never allowed any woman to have.

As the helicopter lifted into the night, he caught a whiff of her scent—that tantalising mix of citrus soap and rose perfume which had beguiled him in the past.

Fierce need dug into his guts as he forced himself to look out into the night. The lights of the mansion glittered as guests milled around the gardens and the terrace and waved at the retreating chopper.

He wouldn't consummate their marriage tonight. They had an eight-hour plane journey on the Cade jet once they got to Heathrow, then a two-hour boat transfer to the island.

He'd arranged for them to have separate bungalows, as per his original promise—which would give him as much time as he needed to get this incessant hunger under control while ensuring that any wayward emotions remained on a tight leash at all times too. So, when he finally took his new bride, he intended it to be on his terms—and at a time of his choosing.

CHAPTER TWELVE

LACEY YAWNED, WOKEN by the bright mid-morning light coming through the luxury beach bungalow's shutters.

She sat up, feeling disorientated, and strangely bereft as the memory of last night's trip to Bermuda came back to her. The short helicopter ride to the airport and the overnight plane journey in Brandon's deluxe private jet. The transfer to a motor yacht on Ireland Island—and the rows of colourful cookie-cutter houses brightened by torch light as they drove from the airport to the port several hours before dawn. The glorious sunrise over the iridescent sea as the launch had skimmed towards the horizon and finally arrived at a wooden dock on a stunning white sand beach. The lavish facilities of the main house—complete with gym, restaurant and large oval swimming pool—and the expertly designed and beautifully appointed bungalows dotted along the beach which had literally taken her breath away.

But, most of all, she remembered Brandon's silence. He'd barely spoken to her and hadn't touched her once since their mind-blowing kiss on the steps of the helicopter before they'd left Wiltshire.

She'd felt branded, owned, after that kiss. But, in the exhausting hours since, she'd been left to feel almost like a discarded toy, a play thing, which Brandon possessed but didn't wish to play with… Yet…

She frowned, her skin prickling alarmingly with that feeling of over-sensitivity. Of hyper-awareness, which he could trigger just by looking at her.

Had he ignored her on purpose? To make her even more aware there was only one thing he wanted from her?

Was this supposed to be another punishment of some sort? Did he expect her to spend the rest of her life atoning for the bad decisions she'd made as a nineteen-year-old? Yes, she'd misjudged Brandon—and his capacity, so far at least, to be a much better father than her own—but she'd been young and scared and she had, in her own misguided way, thought she was protecting her child.

Even if Brandon couldn't forgive her, she had to forgive herself. Or she would turn into that defensive girl again, who had blamed herself because her father couldn't love her.

Brandon was going to have to get past his anger— and learn to trust her. He couldn't blame her for ever. That wasn't healthy for her, or Ruby, or ultimately even for him. And it certainly wasn't a good way to start a life together.

Her pulse jumped. Assuming they had a life together... She swallowed heavily and forced down the ripple of insecurity.

She knew Brandon didn't see this marriage as a lifetime commitment, but as a means to an end. He'd made that abundantly clear more than once. But she'd made the decision to come here, to be with him here alone for the week so she could explore the possibilities, to see if there could be more. And she refused to be put off...or put in her place...

She'd allowed him to have the lavish wedding he'd wanted and had been overwhelmed by the whole process—the highly sought-after wedding planner and her team of designers, florists, caterers et cetera had made her feel as if she'd been playing a role in an elaborate spectacle, rather than being a woman on her wedding day.

Had that been Brandon's intention? To make her aware she had no real place in his life other than the one he had designated for her?

Think again, Cade.

Flinging off the covers, Lacey jumped out of the king-sized bed with a new sense of purpose.

She had no idea where Brandon was. But she had no intention of going in search of him like a lost puppy looking for attention.

The concierge who had showed her round the bungalow early that morning had mentioned a number of the island's natural attractions, including a waterfall only a two-mile walk from the beach.

She began to hunt through the drawers of designer clothes that had been selected for her by a stylist.

Because, apparently, she couldn't even be trusted to dress herself appropriately as Brandon Cade's trophy wife.

After dressing in a ludicrously tiny bikini, a linen beach tunic and some sturdy sandals, and packing a small rucksack with water, sunscreen and mosquito repellent, she set out along the white sand beach.

Her breath caught as sunshine glinted off the turquoise water—a coral reef visible under the translucent sea. A breeze fluttered through the palm trees that edged the sand, refreshing her skin—and reminding her of what it felt like to have Brandon's eyes on her.

A cold swim in a waterfall was just what she needed to take back control of the devil's bargain she'd made with her domineering, overbearing new husband.

Perhaps he didn't plan this to be a real marriage, but she'd be damned if she'd simply fall into step with those plans.

If he thought he'd got himself a convenient wife, this honeymoon would show him that Lacey Carstairs—she caught her breath as she took the path into the island's interior: make that Lacey Cade—was nobody's pushover.

'Where the hell is my wife?' Brandon demanded as he waylaid the concierge at the resort reception.

'I'm sorry, Mr Cade, is she not in her villa?'

'No, she's not,' he said, getting increasingly annoyed. He'd decided to pay a call on her. He'd waited long enough.

Unlike her, he'd chosen not to take a nap to sleep off the jet lag, but had instead gone for a long run on the beach and then spent an hour lifting weights in the on-site gym to take his mind off the sexual frustration—which, instead of being controlled, had only become more explosive during the long journey to the island.

After a shower, he'd headed to her villa. Because she was his wife, and she wanted him just as much as he wanted her. And he was through playing games.

And now this. Where was she?

'The housekeeping staff did mention she wasn't in the villa when they went to clean it an hour ago, sir,' the concierge said.

'An hour ago?' Frustration turned to something that felt disturbingly like panic.

'She seemed interested in Jewel Falls when I mentioned it,' the concierge offered. 'I told her how to get there. Perhaps—'

'Have the boat crew check the coastline,' Brandon interrupted him, the panic scaling down a little. She had probably gone into the interior. But there were a number of coves carved into the rocky headland on the south of the island which could trap the unwary tourist at high tide. The cliffs were a good five miles away—surely Lacey couldn't have got that far? But he wasn't taking any chances.

'Yes, sir,' the concierge said, all but saluting him.

'Would you like me to send a search party to the falls too?'

'No, thanks. I'll head there myself.'

If Lacey was at the falls, he couldn't think of a better place to confront her about her failure to inform him or the staff of her whereabouts, and then give her a hands-on demonstration of her new role as his wife.

And for that he did not want an audience.

Lacey sighed with pleasure, the cold water pounding down from the fissure in the rock wall reinvigorating her hot, sweaty skin. She'd taken her time during the walk, admiring the island's spectacular flora and fauna. But once she'd found the falls she'd been awestruck. Crystal-clear water cascaded from the mossy limestone rocks formed from a volcano—which had built the island's reef millions of years ago, according to the guide book—while its sandy pool nestled in a fragrant grove of hibiscus and oleander.

But she wasn't as interested in the geology now, or the spectacular beauty of her surroundings, as she was in enjoying the tranquil setting and indulging the refreshing feel of the cool water against her skin.

Tipping her head back, she let out one last guttural moan of pleasure before stepping out of the stream. But, as she opened her eyes, she jolted—visceral sensation slamming into her.

The tall, dark figure of her husband stood five feet away, ankle-deep in the water, wearing loose cotton trousers, an open shirt to reveal the tanned contours of his chest and a frown.

Vibrant sensation sank deep into her abdomen under his focussed gaze. Her already pebbled nipples hardened to poke against the skimpy bikini, not from the cold this time, but from the warmth spearing through her body like wildfire. But with the familiar arousal came the swell of emotion.

How long had he been standing there? Watching her?

Tugging a hand out of his pocket, he crooked his finger at her without speaking, directing her to come to him. His movements seemed casual, but the fierce demand in his face was anything but.

She shivered, not from the cold, but from the sharp yank of desire and the tug of annoyance. She slicked the hair back from her face, trying to decide how best to react.

She could refuse to do as he asked. Refuse to allow him to use her as his toy, one he was finally prepared to play with. But that vicious yank—compelling her to do anything and everything he wanted—also made her feel alive…and seen. And she knew denying him would also be to deny herself.

The need twisted into a knot in her abdomen.

He had all the experience here, and she knew how much he liked to dominate and control their sexual encounters—she suspected so he could keep a tight rein on his emotions. But surely, if she was bold, brave and unafraid, she could wrestle some of that power out of his hands?

She walked through the pool towards him, refusing to break eye contact, and stopped a few feet from him.

Exhilaration flowed through her as she noticed the thick ridge of an erection under his trousers. She resisted the urge to cross her arms over her chest.

His dark-green gaze dipped, burning the chill from her wet skin, then fixed back on her face.

'Take it off,' he said, indicating her bikini top.

She sucked in a breath, shocked by the arrogant demand. But, as she steadied her staggered breathing, she acknowledged the delicious thrill charging through her body.

However volatile, however overwhelming, this insistent desire was as much a part of this marriage as the feelings she had begun to nurture and protect. The feelings she hoped one day he might return.

So she looked him in the eye, then forced a smile to her lips—which she hoped looked confident and defiant—and lifted her arms to tug on the string holding the bikini's halter-neck in place.

The bow gave way, releasing the top. She wasn't particularly busty, but her breasts felt heavy, the nipples painfully swollen as she exposed herself to his gaze.

It was his turn to suck in a breath. He looked his fill, the flare of approval, of yearning, in his face like a physical caress leaving a trail of fire in its wake.

When his gaze met hers again, his expression had tightened, tensed, the fierce desire something he was no longer able to control.

'Now take off the rest of it. I want to see all of my wife.'

She shuddered. The emphasis on *my* was deliberately provocative…and possessive.

But still she refused to be cowed, to be intimidated by his need. Or her own. She wanted this, she wanted him. He was the only man she had ever made love to, the only man ever to see her naked. Why should she be embarrassed or ashamed of the silvery marks on her belly left by her pregnancy? Maybe her breasts weren't as pert as they had once been, maybe her hips weren't as narrow, but she was proud of what her body had become to nurture their baby.

Unfortunately, she had never stripped for a man before, and certainly not in the open air, so she completed the striptease with more tenacity than skill. Clumsy fingers released the back hook on the bikini top to let it fall, then she eased off the panties and flung the swatch of fabric onto the bank.

He didn't say anything, didn't speak, as his gaze roamed over her skin. She folded her arms around her waist, lifted her head and stared into his eyes—bold and defiant.

'Now it's your turn,' she managed round the lump of need and terrifying emotion growing in her throat as the wildfire sizzled over her exposed skin. 'I want to see all of my husband too.'

She's magnificent.

Brandon let out a gruff chuckle through dry lips, tantalised by the glorious sight of his wife's naked body—and painfully aroused by her bold request. Need throbbed in his groin, the desire to touch, to taste, all but unbearable ever since he had spotted her standing under the waterfall, her curves glistening and wet, her body barely covered by the strategically placed straps of red fabric.

Ordering her to take off the bikini had been a double-edged sword, because instead of resisting she had met his demands with defiance.

Added to that, the sight of her erect nipples, ruched and reddened by the cold water, the tremble of her breasts as she stripped with unpretentious allure and the trimmed curls covering her sex—where he planned to feast very soon—left him struggling not to explode.

'*Touché,*' he murmured, stripping off his shirt and chucking it on the sand. He unbuttoned the loose cotton trousers, kicking them off to reveal the swimming trunks which could barely contain his painful erection.

Her gaze drifted down and the explosive need pooled in his groin. Reaching out, he tugged her closer.

He couldn't wait any longer.

She gasped as he devoured her neck and licked off the fresh water. Her curves were strong and supple under his hands and he felt her instant response, the moist heat between her thighs, as he explored the swollen folds, torturous and tormenting.

He lifted her easily into his arms and carried her out of the pool, the urgency to bury his length in her tight warmth—to finally claim his wife—something he could no longer control. But, as he placed her on her feet on the bank, she covered the hard ridge in his trunks with her palm, testing the shape and length of him beneath the swimwear.

'You're not naked,' she said, her accusation contradicted somewhat by the vibrant flush on her cheeks—and the devastating desire in her eyes.

'Because I'm about to lose it.' He grasped her wrist, amused by the flare of triumph in her eyes as he brought her marauding fingers to his lips before she won this battle outright.

'Are you on the pill?' he managed.

She nodded.

Thank God.

But, as his lips found the taut nipple and she moaned, her body bowing back, his relief evaporated. He wanted to make another baby with her. Because the thought of seeing for himself the changes to her body as his child grew inside her was even more erotic than watching her strip in front of him, seeing the subtle signs of her previous pregnancy and the uninhibited desire in her eyes.

He recoiled at the vicious wave of arousal that followed.

You need to get inside her before you lose what's left of your sanity.

He turned her to face one of the palm trees that edged the lagoon. Clasping her hips, stroking the silvery scars where his child had marked her, he positioned her and released the massive erection from his trunks.

'Brace yourself,' he murmured against her neck.

She obeyed instinctively, pressing her hands against the trunk as he dragged his fingers through the drenched folds of her sex.

She bucked and sobbed as he circled her swollen clitoris, testing her readiness.

'I need you inside me,' she said. The staggered pants of her breathing, the unequivocal demand, was a siren call to his already fractured senses.

He cupped her breasts to anchor her in place, found the tight entrance to her sex and thrust into her from behind.

She took him to the hilt, her body clamping down hard as she cried out and soared straight to peak.

He held still, the clasp and release of her orgasm, the depth of his penetration in this position, almost more than he could bear.

But, as she began to come down, he started to move, desperate to force her to peak again, stroking a place deep inside he knew would intensify her orgasm.

He kept moving, rolling his hips, gritting his teeth to hold back his own orgasm, determined to claim her, to brand her, to show her she was his. Now and always. But as he struggled to cling on to control the pulse of desperation became overwhelming... and he wasn't sure who was in charge any more. But, what was even much more disturbing, he wasn't sure he cared.

* * *

The brutal pleasure kept intensifying, battering Lacey, driving her to new heights. Each time she got close, he forced her further, turning her into a throbbing mass of sensation.

A sob escaped, but she refused to beg, digging her fingers into the rough tree bark to hold herself steady, to hold herself upright for the deep internal stroking.

He dragged her hair aside to kiss her nape. His hands caressed her heavy breasts, trapping her for the relentless thrusts. So deep, so overwhelming, but never quite enough to take her over again.

But then one hand glided down, stroking over taut sinews, quivering muscles, and located the pulsing centre of her need at last.

'Come for me, Lacey,' he commanded, just as he stroked where their bodies joined.

The wave barrelled through her, splintering pleasure like a tornado, making her shudder and sob.

She heard his grunt of release, the massive erection getting bigger still as he pumped himself into her at last. She was shaking, trembling, as he dragged himself out of her then scooped her shattered body into his arms. But, even as she understood he had destroyed her, she knew she had destroyed him too, his gait uneven, his arms shaking as he carried her into the pool.

They sank together into the cool water to wash off the evidence of their love-making. She flinched, too sore and tender to take the brutal intimacy as he cleaned her.

But she could hear the strain in his voice when he spoke. 'Look at me, Lacey.'

She opened her eyes to focus on him.

'Don't ever go off without telling me where you are again,' he said.

She could see the grooves of strain around his mouth and the muscle flexing in his jaw, as well as the concern in his eyes.

A part of her understood his command was the only way he could articulate to her that he had been worried about her. But, even as her heart opened on the tidal wave of hope, of possibility, another part of her could hear the subtle hint of ownership in his tone and she knew she couldn't let him get away with it.

She drew away from him. 'I'm not a child, Brandon.'

He frowned. 'Yes, but you are my wife.'

She nodded. 'But that doesn't mean I'm obliged to tell you where I am every minute of the day.' Especially as he had tried to treat her on the journey here as little more than a play thing that he could ignore at will.

'Aren't you?' he asked, clasping her wrist to drag her closer and band his arm around her bottom. 'Well, you damn well ought to be.'

Emotion pulsed deep in her chest. Did he feel it too, this brutal connection, the yearning for more?

'This may not be a conventional marriage,' she said, suddenly knowing she had to stand up for herself now, for what this marriage could be, or he would never open himself to her. 'But it is a marriage of equals.'

Maybe it was still the afterglow—the intensity of their lovemaking—which had left her dazzled and disorientated. But even so she cupped his cheek and let the last of her own defences down as she stared into his eyes—and allowed him to see the hope she was trying to keep in perspective. 'If you were worried about me, Brandon, you're allowed to say so. And I'd be happy to put your mind at rest.'

The muscle jumped beneath her palm, but the wary expression on his face only made the emotion pound harder in her chest.

He didn't love her, not yet. It was far too soon for that. For either one of them. They both had insecurities when it came to making themselves vulnerable. She understood that. But, if they were going to have any kind of a marriage, they needed to be honest about their feelings.

His frown deepened, but then he let out a heavy breath and turned his head to press a kiss into her palm. 'Fine,' he said. 'I was worried about you. I didn't know where the hell you were. Is that good enough, Mrs Cade?'

A chuckle popped out of her mouth at his annoyed expression. 'Absolutely, Mr Cade,' she said lightly, euphoria gripping her insides. Then, grasping his broad shoulders, she leapt into his arms.

He swore as they both tumbled backwards into the water together. But when they came up for air, both choking and spluttering, a playful smile danced over his sensual lips.

'You little witch, you nearly drowned us both,' he said. 'I should punish you…'

'You can only punish me if you catch me first!' She yelped, pushing a wave of water into his face.

She danced away from him, shrieking and laughing as he chased her out of the pond. But, when he finally did catch her, the buzz cut glistening with water, the dimple in his cheek winking at her from the stubble on his jaw and his eyes glittering with amused approval, he looked so damn handsome it made her chest ache.

CHAPTER THIRTEEN

'BRANDON, WE NEED to talk about what's going to happen when we return to the UK.' Lacey sliced into the juicy char-grilled tuna steak and tried to keep her voice nonchalant.

But, as her husband lifted his head across the table, the green of his irises flickering with jade fire in the glow of torchlight, and the waves lapping lazily against the nearby shore the only sound, it wasn't easy to ignore the heady pulsing of her heartbeat.

Their honeymoon would be over tomorrow—and it had been nothing short of idyllic. She'd indulged in every pleasure—they'd made love all over the island, as she discovered things about her body she had never known. And she'd thrown herself into every new adventure Brandon had suggested—from snorkelling on the reef, to abseiling into a private cove, to an exhilarating jet-ski safari out to a sand bar where the staff had been waiting to serve them a three-course lunch.

It had bothered her that Brandon had refused to spend the night with her in her bungalow. He'd given her some excuse about not being a good sleeper the night of their mind-blowing tryst at Jewel Falls. But she had been determined not to panic. Patience was the answer. Getting to know her new husband would be a long-term project, because she knew from the little Brandon had confided in her about his past he had been alone for a very long time. He wasn't used to sharing… Not a bed, not a life and certainly not his secrets.

But she knew they had also both been avoiding any difficult conversations about their life together going forward. She'd been okay with that up to now. This week had been a chance to enjoy themselves, to let their guards down, at least a little bit. But when they returned to the UK they'd have some important decisions to make about how their family life would be organised—as she began the mammoth task of reinventing her stalled career.

She couldn't stay in Wiltshire indefinitely. The kind of work she was looking for was mostly based in London. And Ruby had mentioned her old nursery friends that morning during their last video chat— she missed them, and it made sense for her to return to the nursery she loved.

He swallowed, his gaze narrowing. 'What do you wish to discuss?' he said, but he didn't sound pleased at the prospect.

She ignored the foolish blip in her heart rate. This was the kind of conversations a wife had with a husband, and a mother had with the father of her child, something they both needed to learn how to do.

'I got a text from an old colleague at *Splendour* today. Apparently *Buzz* online magazine are looking for a feature writer, and I'm going to apply for it next week.'

He put down his knife and fork, his jaw clenching and his brows flattening into a sharp from. '*Buzz*? Isn't that owned by Roman Garner?'

'He has some shares in it, yes,' she said, not sure why that should be a problem. Garner Media was a rival of Cade Inc, but the small online publication could hardly be seen as a competitor to any of Cade Inc's huge portfolio of news titles.

'Then the answer's no.'

'I'm sorry, what?' Lacey stiffened, shocked, not just by the outrageous statement but the brittle, uncompromising tone.

'You heard me,' he replied. 'I don't want you working for that bastard.' He picked up his cutlery again and sliced neatly into his steak as if the conversation was over.

'I wasn't asking your permission, Brandon,' she said flatly, trying to contain her anger at the dictatorial way he was behaving. 'I was simply letting you know what I plan to do.' Had she been kidding herself about the progress she thought they'd made this week?

It seemed as if she had. When his gaze rose back to her face, the look in his eyes was intractable. Did he really not understand?

'If you want a job, I can find you one at Cade Inc,' he said.

'I can't work at Cade, Brandon. I'm your wife,' she said, her voice rising as she tried to control her indignation.

'So what?' he replied, not budging an inch.

'So everyone would know I got the job because I was married to you. It would make my working relationship with my colleagues untenable, surely you can see that?' she finished, her anger downgrading a notch when he gave her a curt nod.

At last, a concession.

But then he ruined it.

'Fine, how about I buy *Buzz* for you? If you own the title, you being my wife shouldn't be an issue. And you'll be able to decide how much or how little you do.'

'Don't be daft, Brandon.' Was he actually serious right now? 'I appreciate your willingness to do something so...' *Overwhelming, OTT, insane...* 'So generous,' she settled on. Maybe in his own dogmatic, dictatorial way, he was trying to be helpful. 'But I haven't got the experience to own and operate a title like that.'

Nor did she particularly want to. Writing was what she enjoyed. 'And, anyway, you hate celebrity media,' she added, beginning to wonder if she had completely misconstrued his objections to her taking the job with *Buzz*. Was this really just about his dislike of Roman Garner? A need to dictate her role in their marriage? Or something much more fundamental? Because his solution was out of all proportion to a problem that didn't really exist. 'I don't want you to buy me a magazine,' she said. 'I just want to work. My career is important to me.'

'Why?' he said. 'Why isn't being Ruby's mother enough?' he added.

It was her turn to frown at the harsh question, the accusatory tone.

But suddenly she remembered what he had told her about his own mother. Was it possible his objections had nothing to do with Garner, or her need to work, and everything to do with the way his mother had once abandoned him for money?

She heaved a sigh.

'Are you finished eating?' she asked as she stood up. 'Because I'd like to continue this conversation in private.'

The waiting staff was at a discreet distance, but even so she didn't want to have this conversation with them in earshot.

'I'm not going to change my mind,' he said, but followed her and stepped away from the table.

'Let's walk,' she murmured.

She strolled past the torches flickering in the warm island breeze and onto the soft, sandy beach. The sound of the waves lapping lazily against the shore and the soft green glow of phosphorescence shimmering on the surface of the sea seemed impossibly romantic, almost as romantic as the feel of him, tall and indomitable, and so guarded beside her.

The silence stretched out between them as she tried to figure out how best to approach the conversation.

He hated talking about his emotional needs. She got that. She suspected it was because he had spent so much of his life denying he even had any. She'd learnt enough about his dysfunctional relationship with his father, and his lack of a relationship with his mother, to understand why that might be. But she needed him to trust her—as a mother as well as a wife. And to do that he had to forgive her, all the way, for the mistake she'd made in not telling him about Ruby.

And to do *that* he had to understand a lot more about why she'd made that decision. He hadn't asked her for an explanation and she was beginning to realise he probably never would. Because it would mean straying into an emotional landscape he had no experience—and no desire—to navigate. So she would have to make this move, for both of them.

'Can we talk openly?' she said at last.

'I suppose so,' he said, but she could hear the edge in his voice.

She had to let her own guard down, to let him see she had scars too. It was way past time she told him the truth she had recently discovered, about why she hadn't told him about Ruby much sooner. That her silence hadn't just been a result of that naive girl's insecurity, but also her broken relationship with her own father.

'I just want you to know that I know exactly what it feels like to have a father who's an absolute jerk…' she began.

* * *

Brandon saw the familiar compassion darken Lacey's eyes. And he recoiled against it instinctively. How had they ended up talking about his father?

'Mine walked out when Milly and I were still too young to remember him,' she added gently, the quiet, pragmatic tone somehow all the more powerful because it was so carefully devoid of sentiment. 'And he never returned,' she continued. 'We discovered after Mum died that he had another family. Sons he was proud of, a wife he loved when we contacted him after my mother's funeral. He didn't want to know us—which I guess was why my mum avoided conversations about him when we were kids. But she had always made it clear to us his failings were not ours. That just because he couldn't love us it didn't make us less than. Something I realised recently, I had always struggled to accept.'

She sighed. 'I'm just incredibly sad you never had that from your own mum. Having two selfish bastards for parents was really bad luck.'

He stared at her, the strange pulsing in his chest turning into something disturbing. He hadn't asked about her past for two specific reasons—it would increase the intimacy between them, and he had no desire to reveal more of his own. But something about the way she spoke of her father, without bitterness, without regret, seemed incredibly brave.

'How old were you both, when your mother died?' he asked, curious about something he had tried hard not to care about.

'Milly was fifteen, I had just turned eighteen.'

'That must have been tough,' he said, remembering her as she had been at nineteen—eager and erudite, ambitious and smart, and already on a fast track within Cade Inc's internship programme. Of course, he hadn't realised at the time she was still a teenager, and had assumed she was several years older because of her confidence when she'd flirted with him.

But why hadn't he ever confronted his own culpability that night? Why hadn't he ever considered how vulnerable she had been?

She shrugged. 'Luckily, social services were happy to declare me as Milly's guardian. And I already had the internship at Cade Inc lined up.'

'Which I destroyed for you,' he said abruptly.

He had tried to get over his resentment about her refusal to tell him about Ruby when she became pregnant. But the truth was, he'd been happy to dismiss his own actions. And he had never once asked about her circumstances. Had never considered she was the sole breadwinner for her and her sister. Had never felt any guilt about the fact he'd left her pregnant and jobless as a direct result of his own carelessness.

Why had he never checked up on her to make absolutely sure there had been no consequences?

'That was a mistake,' she said, giving him leeway he now knew he didn't deserve. 'You didn't destroy my career on purpose.'

'Dammit, Lacey, you were a virgin and only nineteen. I knew the condom had failed and yet I never contacted you to be sure you were okay.'

She blinked, clearly taken aback by his outburst, which only made him feel like more of a bastard.

'If it hadn't split, we wouldn't have Ruby, so I'd say it's a moot point.'

'Even so, I owe you an apology,' he said tightly, finally saying what he should have said when he'd first discovered Ruby's existence.

'Okay.' She nodded slowly, her eyes glowing with an emotion he didn't really understand…and wasn't sure he wanted to understand. 'Apology accepted, but it doesn't mean much if you can't forgive me.' She turned towards him in the moonlight, the breeze blowing in her hair and making it dance around her face. She looked so young and earnest…and brave in that moment, he felt something shift and break open inside him.

'What for?' he asked, hopelessly confused now.

'I made a terrible mistake not telling you about Ruby. I didn't trust you, but I can see now a lot of the way I reacted was all wrapped up in the way my father had rejected me and Milly. I blamed you for what he did. I didn't even know you. And yet I judged you. I assumed you would be a terrible father. And that wasn't fair.'

He frowned, feeling strangely threatened by the forthright apology, her easy acceptance of the way he had behaved. 'I was an arrogant, entitled bastard that night, let's be honest, which might also have had something to do with why you kept Ruby from me.'

Why was she letting him off the hook so easily?

She squeezed his hand, a smile spreading across her face. 'True,' she said, with a complete lack of anger. 'But I was a clueless idiot, so I would say we're even. And, if you can forgive me, I can certainly forgive you.'

He turned his hand over to link his fingers with hers, the need to touch her suddenly about more than just sex, more than just the intense physical connection which he had exploited so vociferously in the last seven days.

She'd met every one of his demands with demands of her own. And he'd enjoyed the time he spent with her—not just in bed, but out of it too. Lacey had a playful, adventurous nature which intrigued and excited him. And in the last seven days, as she had spoken at length about their daughter, he had come to realise what a good mother she was too. Patient, supportive but also fascinated and amused by Ruby, despite the circumstances of her birth.

'I know you don't trust people easily, Brandon,' she said as she held onto his hand. 'And I think now I know why—because the people you should have been able to trust as a little boy both let you down horribly. You asked me why being Ruby's mum isn't enough for me, and I want you to know that it absolutely is. I love her with everything I am, and everything I'm ever going to be, but I don't see being a mother and a career woman being mutually exclusive,' she continued. 'I know I can do both. And I want you to trust me on that, if you can.'

He tensed, drawing his fingers out of hers as the crack in his chest threatened to become a chasm.

'Okay,' he said, his voice thick with an emotion he did not want to feel, was determined not to feel ever again. He did trust her, he realised, perhaps much more than he should. How had that happened without him even realising it?

Because it made him think of that young boy who had begged his father for affection—for so long—and had never received it.

He wasn't that kid any more. But the thought of her being able to see that boy scared him. Because that boy could be hurt.

Placing his free hand on her waist, he tugged her into the lee of his body, letting her feel the erection which was never far away. 'Although I'm not sure what any of this has to do with you working for Roman Garner,' he said gruffly.

He didn't want her working for Garner, for the simple reason she was his. Eventually she would figure out there was a limit to what he could offer her. But he intended to ensure she was bound to him by then, in every way that mattered.

She smiled, then rubbed against him, making the erection harden. 'I just wanted to establish that this is a partnership, Brandon. One in which we can both get what we want. If we're open with each other.' She grinned, the sparkle of affection in her eyes as spellbinding as it was disturbing.

Grasping his hand, she drew him towards her cabin, making his heart beat a hasty tattoo against his ribs. She was taking the initiative, and for once he felt no need to fight it as arousal roared in his gut.

This is about sex, and making a home together for the child you share. Nothing more. Nothing less.

He climbed the wooden steps in silence, clasping her hips as she threw her arms around his neck and stretched up on tiptoes to capture his lips. He drove his tongue into her mouth on her sob of need, but let her lead the dance of temptation and retreat. Let her feast as the hunger raced through his blood. He needed to have her, to keep her, by whatever means necessary.

But as they made love, first fast and furious on her bed, then slow and easy in the rainfall shower—and she gave him everything, while holding nothing back—he kept that hidden, vulnerable part of himself ruthlessly in check.

Because he was never going to give anyone the power to hurt him again.

But, as he lay in her bed hours later, he listened to the low hum of the cicadas outside and the soft murmurer of her breathing and struggled to close the chasm in his chest the only way he knew how.

Lacey felt Brandon shift in the bed beside her and forced her eyelids to open, her exhausted body still humming from the intensity of their love-making. But, as Brandon eased her out of his arms and threw off the sheet, she reached out to grasp his arm.

'Brandon, where are you going?' she murmured,

hating the neediness in her voice, but hating the hollow ache under her ribs more.

Was he leaving her bed *again*? *Tonight*? Why? When she had been sure they had made so much progress?

He glanced down at her, his hand covering hers, before his thumb skimmed down her arm. 'You're still awake?' he said, his voice gruff. Her heartbeat accelerated, the warm, seductive touch triggering an instant response in her abdomen. 'I thought I had exhausted you.'

It wasn't an answer, but she forced herself to let go of him.

'You did,' she said, flopping back onto the bed. 'Were you going to your own cabin?' she asked. 'You don't need to,' she added. Did he still think she would hold him to that asinine promise about separate bedrooms after everything they'd shared this week? 'I'd like to wake up with you in the morning.'

He chuckled, but the laugh sounded strained somehow. Evasive...? Or was this her insecurity talking again?

'You're insatiable,' he said.

This wasn't about sex, or not just about sex, not to her. She wasn't even sure she could have sex again, after all the times he'd had her that night already.

But, when he relaxed back onto the pillows and pulled her into his embrace, she let herself sink into his arms. The moment seemed fragile somehow and, while she didn't want to push, she also didn't want to let him go, not tonight. Because she was desperately afraid she was falling in love with him.

His fingers threaded through her hair, hooking the unruly curls behind her ear. He pressed his lips to her temple.

'I've been thinking,' he said, his voice a soft rumble in the still night. 'Why don't you stop taking the contraceptive pills when we get back to the UK?'

'W-what?' She jolted upright, wide awake now, so shocked by the suggestion, she wasn't even sure she'd heard it correctly.

His palm covered her belly over the sheet, rubbing seductively. His gaze when it met hers again was dark with arousal, but also full of possessiveness. And her heart jumped into her throat.

'Ruby will be five in a few months, and I don't want her to be an only child,' he said, his voice forceful now, and thick with purpose. 'I've been one my whole life, and believe me, it sucks,' he added. But then his hand settled on her belly, making the skin prickle and throb. 'Plus I want the chance to see you pregnant with my child,' he said, the passion in his tone as disturbing as the intensity. The leap in her pulse, and the blast of hope, was as terrifying as it was exciting. Surely he wouldn't suggest such a thing if he didn't think their marriage had a future?

His thumb cruised up to circle her nipple and make it ache.

'I can't think of anything more erotic,' he said.

For a moment she was speechless, sucked under the tidal wave of longing he could exploit so easily.

But this wasn't just a longing for physical pleasure any more, not for her—it was so much more than that. It was a longing for his approval, his love.

She trapped his hand against her breast. She mustn't get ahead of herself, not again, not the way she had as a girl of nineteen before she'd been dumped so cruelly. Not least because there was so much more at stake now.

He wanted her. He might even need her. She got that. She was beyond flattered, and stupidly touched that he would want to have more children with her. But she couldn't let herself get carried away by the giddy hope making her heart pulse and pound in her chest.

'Can I think about it?' she asked, knowing she already wanted to have more children with him, but knowing neither of them were ready to have them yet. 'We've only been married for a week,' she added, to cover the brutal swelling in her chest.

She wanted this to work. She wanted to have a future with him. But was that really what he was offering?

He let out a rueful laugh. 'Sure,' he said. He tucked her back against his side. 'Now, go to sleep, we have to leave early in the morning. And we need to find a place for us to live back in London. If that's what you want?'

She nodded and yawned, settling back into bed, loving the feel of him beside her. And beyond happy that he seemed willing for them to live in the city. Together.

When she awoke the next morning, she found him

gone again. But this time she convinced herself it had to be the flight that had torn him from her side in the early hours.

And when they returned to the UK, and he told her he had arranged to buy a gated mansion in Islington so Ruby could return to her old nursery—and he could spend more time with his daughter—she convinced herself it didn't matter if he still couldn't stay the night in her bed. Or that they never seemed to get much quality time alone together—unless they were busy tearing each other's clothes off.

Surely greater intimacy, more trust, would grow in time? She just needed to be patient.

And why did it have to be a bad thing she was falling in love with this hard, indomitable man when he was also her husband? And the father of her child?

CHAPTER FOURTEEN

One month later

'BRANDON, DO YOU have a minute?' Lacey asked breathlessly, overjoyed to find her husband in his study for once, having rushed back after dropping Ruby at nursery to catch him before he left for the day. She had exciting news she could not wait to share.

'Actually, yes, I wanted to talk to you too,' Brandon said, closing his laptop. Lacey's excitement downgraded a little as she spotted the rigid expression on his face. Was something wrong?

After all, it was unusual to find him still at home when she got back in the mornings.

She dismissed the blip of panic.

For goodness' sake, stop freaking out. That's old, insecure Lizzy Devlin talking, not new, loved-up Lacey Cade who now has a brand-new dream job to go with her new improved marriage.

She had been forced to put her job hunt on the back burner ever since they had returned from Bermuda, while she'd concentrated on the move and getting her daughter back into some semblance of a routine. But she'd interviewed for the position at *Buzz* over a video link yesterday afternoon and had received a call ten minutes ago, while she'd been walking back from the nursery, to say she'd got the job.

She was hoping Brandon would be excited too, despite his earlier misgivings. After all, she'd come to terms with the fact she'd fallen hopelessly in love with him in the last four weeks. And watching him fall in love with his daughter—and Ruby fall in love with him—and seeing them begin to form a strong, sweet bond together had only made her love him more.

Having Brandon fall in love with her too was always going to be a long-term project. But he was already an integral part of both her and Ruby's lives. And the sex was amazing. Brandon was a dominant but generous lover who liked to push her boundaries, while also being supremely sensitive to her needs. And she'd adored every second of exploring and exploiting their kinetic physical connection.

It still bothered her that each night, after she fell asleep in his arms, exhausted, he would slip away from her to sleep in his own room. And each morning she would wake up alone again. But she was determined not to freak out about that either. She knew he had trust issues. And, even if they hadn't discussed it again since that magical night on their honeymoon, she felt sure it was only a matter of time before he opened up the rest of the way.

'Fab, me first, because I have some wonderful news,' she said.

At exactly the same time, Brandon said, 'I understand you've been offered the job at *Buzz*.'

'Um…y-yes,' she stammered, more than a little deflated he'd stolen her surprise. 'How did you find out? They only told me ten minutes ago.'

'That's beside the point,' he said, but something sparked in his eyes which she couldn't read—because it looked weirdly like irritation. 'I thought we agreed you weren't going to work there,' he said. It wasn't a question.

'When did we agree to that?' she replied carefully. Why was he looking at her like that? As if she'd done something wrong? This wasn't just annoyance, it was disapproval.

'I thought we were having another child,' he said, his gaze becoming flat and remote, his tone accusatory. 'You said you would think about it. But I found out this morning you just got prescribed another six months' supply of contraceptive pills.'

Shock came first, swiftly followed by anger, but right beneath it was that dropping sensation in her stomach. That brutal, unrelenting feeling of inadequacy she remembered so well from the last time she had seen her father the day after their mother's funeral, when he had told Milly and her ever so politely that, while he was sorry for their loss, he had another family now and he simply did not have time to deal with their problems.

'How do you know about my prescription?' she

demanded, wanting to be angry but unable to muster anything past the ball of misery in her stomach.

'I found the pills in your bathroom cabinet,' he said, striding round his desk, the look on his face making it clear he believed he was the injured party. 'After I heard about your job offer.'

The hope she had been nurturing for over a month—ever since that beautiful night in his arms in Bermuda—died slowly inside her as he continued.

'We had a deal, Lacey. You asked me to trust you, and I did. Then you applied for that damn job behind my back.' Something flickered in his eyes that looked almost like hurt. But how could she even think that, when she had been wrong about so much else?

She'd thought they were building something important here, that he was starting to fall in love with her. But his approval had always been conditional, she suddenly realised, on never crossing that line in the sand he had drawn between them.

'You had no right to check up on my prescription,' she managed. 'And there's no reason I can't have a job *and* a baby.' She shook her head, the brutal yearning in her chest mocking her. 'But that's not even the point. I said I would think about it, but it's clear now I'd be a fool to consider having another child with you.'

'Why the hell not?' he said, the temper in his voice upsetting her even more.

He hadn't opened himself to her, opened himself to the possibility of love. Not really. She'd hardly seen him in the last four weeks, except when he'd wanted to sleep with her, and even then he refused to spend the night with her. Why had she been so ready to accept that? To accept the crumbs of his affection, rather than demanding more?

'Because I'm not ready to bring another child into a marriage that obviously isn't working,' she said, the words hurting her throat.

His expression went from sharp to fierce. 'Of course it's working,' he said. 'We're making a good home here for our child. *Together.* I want you. I can't stop wanting you. And you want me. What the heck else is there?'

'Love.' She blurted the word out, hating how needy it sounded.

'Love?' The astonished expression only crucified her more.

She hugged herself, her heart splintering in her chest. 'I've fallen in love with you, Brandon,' she murmured, finally telling him the truth she should have told him weeks ago. But she had never imagined telling him like this. She had thought it would be a declaration full of promise, possibility and excitement. Instead it felt cloying and pathetic, when he simply stared at her, his expression blank.

He looked genuinely stunned, but then his gaze intensified, holding something she didn't understand. 'If you love me,' he said slowly, his voice rough with an emotion she didn't understand, because it sounded almost like regret, 'Why won't you have another child with me?'

She stared at him, her whole body beginning to shake—sadness and longing making the boulder in her stomach grow. 'Because you don't love me back, Brandon. And I'm not even sure you're capable of loving me back any more.'

Brandon swallowed down the panic threatening to consume him.

He couldn't lose her. Not now, not after discovering what a life with her and Ruby...and hopefully more children...would be like.

Each night he made love to her with a fury, a desperation, he hoped would bind her to him for ever. But, as soon as he watched her go over, his desperation only got worse.

He understood why she wanted to work. But he didn't want her working for that libidinous bastard Roman Garner.

He'd been thinking about Lacey having another baby ever since the night he had suggested it in Bermuda, the erotic thought morphing into something so much more compelling.

It was the perfect solution.

Sex would never be enough to bind a woman like her—full of fire, passion and honesty—to a man like him, but he had hoped that a baby...a new life they could share in this time...would be enough.

And now he'd blown it.

She wanted love. But he could never give her that. Because he simply didn't know how to love. Even the thought of letting his guard down to that extent made the anxiety build like a tsunami—and took him back to all those times in his father's study when he had yearned for one single sign of affection or approval, only to have his childish hopes destroyed.

Sure, he could fake it, tell her what she wanted to hear. But he knew she was far too emotionally intelligent not to see through it.

'I don't want you working for Roman Garner,' he managed, trying to keep the panic out of his voice. If she knew how much he needed her to be here every time he came home in the evening, and when he left in the morning, she would use it against him.

She stared at him, her eyes sheened with an emotion that reached into his chest and gave a hard yank.

Disappointment.

The feeling of inadequacy, of confusion, churned in his gut—reminding him far too forcefully of that lost, needy kid.

'You're my wife and he's a rival,' he added stiffly, to try and distance himself from that boy and turn himself back into the man he had become… A man who never let the fear and insecurity which had dogged him throughout his childhood show.

'We can revisit the question of another baby when you're more amenable.' He let his gaze sweep over her figure to settle on her belly in the jeans she wore, the fierce desire to see their child grow there all but overwhelming.

She blinked slowly, the sadness in her eyes only making the storm in his gut pitch and roll.

Ignore it. You can't give her what she wants. You

know it. And eventually she will realise it too, and will hopefully be prepared to live within those parameters.

'This isn't about the job, Brandon, or another baby. This is about what you're prepared to give to this marriage. To give to me.'

It was hardly the concession he'd been looking for.

'I want you here with me, in my life, as my wife and the mother of my children. Why isn't that enough?'

If she wasn't ready to have another child...*yet*... he'd have to compromise and find her a job at Cade Inc, he thought frantically.

'And yet you still can't spend the night in my bed,' she said, her eyes sheened with unshed tears.

'I told you, I'm not a good sleeper, I'd wake you up.' The anxiety he remembered so well from his childhood—coupled with the cruel realisation he could never do enough, never *be* enough, to make anyone truly care for him—gripped his throat. He couldn't give her that, couldn't let her see him at his most vulnerable.

'And I've told you I don't care,' she replied. 'You have to let your barriers down, to let me in. To let me know you. Why does that terrify you so much?'

'I'm not good with that much intimacy...' he said, but even he could hear the cowardice in his words, the note of panic and desperation, and realised how pathetic he sounded.

Could she hear it too? She must be able to. But, instead of calling him out on it, she brushed away the single tear that flowed down her cheek. 'Then we don't have a real marriage, Brandon. And a real marriage is what I want.'

And then she turned and left him standing alone in the study. He stood there for what felt like an eternity, the walls closing in around him, trying to shore up all the defences he'd worked so hard to build over so many years.

At last, anger flowed over the panic, inadequacy and fear. She would come around. This was what they'd agreed to—she couldn't change the terms of their agreement after only one month. And what about Ruby? What about the daughter she'd denied him? She owed him this marriage.

But, as he strode out of the study and out of the house, he could already feel his mind working, desperately trying to come up with a plan to fill up the huge, empty hole opening up all over again in his gut. And threatening to swallow him whole.

CHAPTER FIFTEEN

'WHY DIDN'T DADDY come home tonight?' Ruby yawned, the sleepy question making Lacey's heart hurt.

'I told you, baby, he had to work late, but he'll make it up to you tomorrow. Daryl says Daddy has bought tickets to take you to the zoo, just the two of you.'

The text from Daryl had arrived twenty minutes ago, saying he had purchased the tickets at Brandon's request and informing her of her husband's plans.

As soon as Lacey had read the text, though, it had reminded her of the curt demands she had received from Daryl when Brandon had first found out about his daughter.

And she had known the decision to contact her through his assistant, not to return home tonight, was deliberate. Brandon was avoiding her and the messy emotional demands she'd made that morning.

She'd been drained and on edge all day. The last of the hope she had relied on for four weeks dying as she went through every aspect of their conversation that morning over and over again. And she knew she hadn't read any of it wrong.

She'd asked him to love her, at least to try to love her, and he'd refused.

Where did they go from here?

'*Really*, Mummy?' Ruby said, her eyes brightening with excitement. 'Can Daddy and me spend the whole day there? I love the zoo.'

A day spent with her father all to herself was Ruby's ultimate gift and Lacey refused to spoil it. But as she tucked her daughter into bed, and finally got her to go to sleep, she knew she had some tough decisions to make.

She couldn't stay in a marriage with a man who refused to open himself to at least the possibility of love. Because it would destroy her in the end, and bring back that girl who had once believed she was the problem, the reason her father couldn't love her.

The staff had the night off on Friday—which was usually an excuse for Brandon and her to make love on the living room rug. But tonight she made herself a simple dinner alone in the kitchen.

She glanced at her phone to check the time.

Where was he? Wasn't he going to come home at all tonight?

After finishing the food and loading the dishwasher, she poured herself a glass of wine and waited in the sitting room. As the hours ticked by, her hopelessness and confusion increased, but with it came determination.

Brandon was a man who she suspected had never

had his defences tested. Had never had to bend since his father's death. But he would have to bend now or she would be forced to give him an ultimatum.

She couldn't live without love. She understood if he couldn't love her yet. But she had to know if he intended them to be bound by nothing more than their daughter…and their sexual connection…always. Because that wasn't enough, not for her.

She'd begun to doze off when she jerked awake to find his dark shape filling the doorway.

'Lacey?' he murmured. 'You're still up?'

He sounded surprised, which made the hurt pulse in her chest.

'Of course. I wanted to speak to you about our conversation this morning,' she said.

He strode across the room to grasp her hands and pull her out of the chair. But then his lips descended on hers to devour her mouth like a starving man.

The kiss was dark, demanding, possessive—triggering the instant wave of arousal she couldn't stop. But she stumbled back, out of his grasp, folding her arms around her waist to stop the shivers of response.

'It's no good, Brandon, it won't work any more. We can't fill the holes in our marriage with sex.'

She had expected him to seduce her, had expected him to argue, demand, coerce, coax so that he could get what he wanted. But instead he jerked backwards, then sat down heavily on the couch and sunk his fingers into his hair.

'I know,' he murmured.

It was the very last thing she had expected him to

say. But suddenly she noticed the stoop of his shoulders, the grooves in his short hair, as if he'd run his fingers through it many times.

He looked up at her then and she saw the turmoil in his eyes he could no longer disguise.

'If you want to take the job with Garner, you can,' he said, his voice hoarse. 'I won't object. And we can wait as long as you need to talk about having another child.' He sounded broken and desperately unhappy.

She sat next to him, lost for words. This wasn't about the job, or the possibility of more children. But she could see how hard these concessions had been for him to make, and finally she began to understand why. This wasn't about controlling her. It was about controlling his own need.

'Just…' He cleared his throat. 'Just please don't leave me.'

She heard it then, the echo of pain and fear, of insecurity, and suddenly she understood what he was doing. He was bargaining with her for her affection, the way she suspected he must have once bargained with his father and his mother.

She placed a hand on his thigh and felt the muscle tense beneath her palm. And let her heart melt. 'I'm not like them, Brandon.'

His head jerked round. 'What do you mean?'

'I won't leave you if we have a disagreement. Or if I don't get what I want. Marriage is a negotiation, and I'm sure we'll have lots more disagreements in our future. But it's also about love. About the freedom to make your own choices.' She took in a deep breath.

He'd come to her—he'd tried to fix this and that meant a lot. Maybe she hadn't been wrong after all. Maybe he could love her, but he just didn't know how to show it.

'I know it's scary,' she said. 'I was scared to love you too. But what I'm giving you is a gift, with no strings attached. I won't take it away, use it against you, the way they did. Because I love you, and they never did. All I'm asking is that you open yourself to the possibility of love in return.'

She breathed the words, her heart shattering when he stiffened and stood up. He swore under his breath and marched across to the room's fireplace to stare into the empty hearth.

She sat still, but her heart broke for him when his reply sliced through the silence. Because what she heard in his voice wasn't anger, or even demand, it was despair.

'You don't know what you're asking of me,' Brandon said, his jaw tight, his whole body rigid with the need to hold firm against the emotion in her voice.

He'd agreed to her terms. Why couldn't that be enough to make her stay?

'What are you so scared of, Brandon?' The quiver of vulnerability in her tone, the emotion, sank its claws into his resolve, tearing through the last of his reserves, the last of his control.

He shook his head, his whole body trembling now as the emotion he didn't know how to stop battered him.

He sunk his hands into his pockets and tried to brace himself against the swell of panic, of fear. But it did no good, because he was back in his father's study again. He was that forlorn, desperate child, terrified to be alone, but even more terrified to let himself ask for more when he knew it would never be given to him.

A hand settled on his back, spreading warmth through his system and burning through the chill.

'What is it, Brandon? If you told me, maybe we could fix it.'

We.

Could it really be that easy? The cynic in him said no way, but there was enough of that lonely child inside him to turn and look at her. To gauge her reaction.

She gazed at him, those chestnut eyes rich with an emotion he had been determined to dismiss that morning but wanted so badly to believe now.

'How can you love me?' he said, the broken child talking now inside the man. The child he had silenced for so long, it hurt to know he had always been there, lurking, waiting, needing.

A lone tear ran down her cheek. 'Oh, Brandon,' she said as she brushed it away with her fist.

She reached up and clasped his cheeks to drag his mouth down to hers.

But as he gripped her waist, desperate to kiss her, she whispered against his lips, 'I love you because you forgave me for the terrible mistake I made in not telling you about your child.' She searched his face and he realised she could see him as no one else ever had. Could see his flaws and his weaknesses, as well as his strengths, and it didn't disgust her.

'I love you because you were determined to be Ruby's father even though you didn't know how.' Her eyes glowed, full of compassion and affection, resolve and tenacity, but most of all full of love.

'I love you for all the things you are—a father, a lover, a husband—and all the things you can be, if you'll just open your heart again.' She smiled, the rich dark amber full of new hope. 'And let me in too, as well as Ruby.'

He felt the answering glow in his heart melting the block of ice which had been there for so long, stopping him from feeling.

It hurt to be this vulnerable. To be this unsure.

But she was right. He loved his child. Why should loving Lacey be so difficult when everything about her fascinated and excited him, captivated and beguiled him? Her strength, her intelligence, her bravery and even her total refusal to let him hide from his own feelings, or hers.

He touched his forehead to hers and let out an unsteady breath, his hands sliding under her T-shirt to caress the warm skin beneath.

She was really here, and she would stay. No matter what. But...

'I want to love you,' he managed, the words rough, rusty, the commitment terrifying even now. 'But I can't...' He wrapped his arms around her, crushing her to him. 'I can't bear to lose you. And I'm bound to screw this up from time to time,' he whispered against her neck, burying his face into the soft spray of curls, breathing in the sweet, erotic scent of roses. 'So you have to promise me...'

He huffed out a breath and drew back, feeling foolish, needy, even a bit pathetic, but knowing he had to ask, to be sure. 'You'll let me know if I mess up. That you won't walk away without giving me a chance to fix it.'

Lacey stared at this big, bold, indomitable man, heard the vulnerability in his voice and knew he loved her. Maybe he couldn't say it yet. Maybe he didn't really even know it yet. But he would, eventually.

She had hope now and security. But most of all she understood why he had tried so hard to hold himself back. Because he was even more terrified than she was.

'I'm not like him, Brandon,' she said again, letting him see everything inside her—all the love, the fear, the hope and the longing. Letting him know that they were equals. Always.

'He didn't deserve you. But Ruby and I...' She grinned as she took his hand and pressed it against her belly. 'And any other babies we have...eventually,' she added because, as much as she wanted to have more children with this man, children they could watch grow together, she also wanted more time with just the three of them. 'We *do* deserve you.'

'I hope you know I consider that a binding agreement—which I will require in writing, Mrs Cade,' he murmured, only half-joking.

She laughed, the joy in her heart creating a heady ache that was still scary but so right. 'I'll sign anything you want, Mr Cade,' she replied. 'But only if you sign it too.'

He lifted her up and held her aloft, his gruff chuckle joining her laughter, then let her body slide down against his, making her tantalisingly aware of the hard ridge thrusting against her belly through their clothing.

'Count on it,' he murmured, then proceeded to strip her naked and seal the deal with the ruthless efficiency she adored.

EPILOGUE

One year later

'DADDY, IS THE baby all cooked now, then?' Ruby bounced on Brandon's hip as he strode down the hospital corridor. His daughter looked as if she were ready to explode with excitement.

He knew the feeling. After leaving Lacey and his brand-new baby son in the exclusive private maternity hospital in Mayfair at 3:00 a.m. that morning, his heart had been ticking over so fast he'd been sure he might never sleep again this decade.

As it happened, he'd crashed out as soon as his head had dropped onto the bed he now shared with Lacey all night, every night—thanks to her unstinting love and support, and the hours of therapy he had finally admitted he needed to get over the fear of intimacy he had developed in childhood...

The same bed which had felt so empty over the past two days since Lacey had gone into hospital for observation. And their son had decided to put in a scarily hasty appearance three weeks ahead of schedule.

The glorious dreams of his son's tiny mouth latching onto his wife's breast for the first time had swirled in and out of his exhausted brain, chased by the terrifying nightmares of six far too fast, but also never-ending, hours of pain and fear as Lacey had laboured like a pro and he'd completely fallen to pieces inside while trying not to show it.

'Yes, he's all cooked and ready to meet you now, Rubes,' he said, suddenly grateful he had not had to go through the labour experience twice.

His daughter meant so much to him—and he would always regret the four years he'd missed watching her grown into the bright, brilliant nearly six-year-old she was now—but her actual birth, not so much.

One thing was for sure—no way on earth was he touching her mother again until they had had a serious conversation about effective methods of contraception. He couldn't get the picture out of his head of her in agonising pain as the contractions had hit in waves. Which should take at least a decade.

Funny to think he'd been desperate to get her pregnant when they'd first been married. But he had been totally okay with waiting, once their marriage had morphed into something real, beautiful and so full of promise and possibilities, it made him ache.

He told her he loved her now every chance he got but, much more importantly, he knew she believed him.

Lacey challenged him and provoked him, excited and fascinated him, always. But, as well as being a wife and a lover, she was also his best friend and the woman he couldn't wait to share every new adventure with. She—and Ruby—filled up all the holes in his life he'd thought could never be filled for so long, and he couldn't wait for the new baby to add another layer of joy and insanity to that glorious chaos.

He'd taken a back seat in his business for the last year—finally forced to acknowledge that so much of his relentless drive and ambition had been linked to the subconscious need to impress a dead man. He still loved his work, and he hadn't entirely given up on expanding Cade Inc into the US market, but he didn't work seven days a week any more. He took school holidays off now, and weekends, and happily played hooky from work to hang out with Ruby if Lacey had a feature to finish or an interview to do. He had even got into the habit of showing off his wife at the sort of media parties and society events he had once despised.

His life had become rich and full, something he would never have envisaged it being. Because for the first time ever he'd discovered what true happiness actually felt like. Not sealing a deal with a media conglomerate in Spain, or launching a new cable news channel in Kenya—but spending a sun-kissed day mucking about with his daughter on a beach in Bermuda, or snatching a make-out session with his heavily pregnant wife in the shower before his chatterbox daughter and her nutty dog bounded into his bedroom to turn the chaos right back up to eleven.

When Lacey had fallen pregnant by accident eight months ago—a result of a stomach bug messing with her contraceptives—he'd actually been more shocked than overjoyed. Had they really been ready to take this step now?

But, as he'd watched Lacey's slim figure ripen with their child, he'd discovered the process was at least every bit as erotic as he'd thought it would be.

As he shoved open the door to Lacey's hospital room, and Ruby wriggled out of his arms to dash across to her mother, he stopped in the doorway to take in the scene—and stamp it on his memory for ever. His wife cradled their new-born in a chair by the bed, the light from the window gilding her soft curls and the tiny bundle in her arms as she lowered them to introduce Ruby to her brother.

His heart took another direct hit—one of so many over the last year—and felt as if it had stopped beating for several seconds as he absorbed the tableau they made.

Doesn't matter if you're ready, Cade. This is it. This is everything. Scary, yeah—terrifying, even. But also the only thing that will ever really matter.

Then Lacey's gaze connected with his as Ruby began chattering a mile a minute to her brother. Poor kid—he was unlikely to get a word in edgeways for the foreseeable future. Good thing he couldn't talk.

His wife smiled, her expression tired but so happy. And his heart kicked back into gear and began to beat double time.

'Hello, Mr Cade,' Lacey said. 'I hope you guys have come to bust us out of here, because Junior and I are ready to go home.'

Home. A word which had meant nothing to him for so long and now meant everything.

His heart expanded as he strolled to his wife and lifted the now fussy baby out of her arms—his son looked somewhat indignant at being so rudely awakened by his inquisitive big sister.

Welcome to my world, kid.

He leant down to whisper to Lacey, 'Why do you think I brought my accomplice with me?' Then— because how could he resist kissing that gorgeous mouth?—he touched his lips to hers.

She opened for him as she always did, tempting him deeper and taking the kiss to a sweet, sultry place. It occurred to him, as the familiar heat settled in his groin, that not making love to his wife again for a decade might be a bit too much of a punishment for both of them. Perhaps a year of abstinence would have to do.

They were forced to break the kiss when Ruby started making 'yuck, yuck' noises, and the baby in his arms began crying and fretting in earnest.

He chuckled as his wife's smile turned into a

knowing grin and the steady beat of joy, happiness and fulfilment—which he'd become so comfortable with over the last year—settled back into his heart.

'Time to get our kids home, Mrs Cade,' he murmured.

And let the chaos continue.

* * * * *

If you were blown away by the drama in
Revealing Her Best Kept Secret
then why not explore these other
Heidi Rice stories?

The Billionaire's Proposition in Paris
The CEO's Impossible Heir
Banished Prince to Desert Boss
A Baby to Tame the Wolfe
Unwrapping His New York Innocent

Available now!

#4081 REUNITED BY THE GREEK'S BABY
by Annie West

When Theo was wrongfully imprisoned, ending his affair with Isla was vital for her safety. Proven innocent at last, he discovers she's pregnant! Nothing will stop Theo from claiming his child. But he must convince Isla that he wants her, too!

#4082 THE SECRET SHE MUST TELL THE SPANIARD
The Long-Lost Cortéz Brothers
by Clare Connelly

Alicia's ex, Graciano, makes a winning bid at a charity auction to whisk her away to his private island. She must gather the courage to admit the truth: after she was forced to abandon Graciano...she had his daughter!

#4083 THE BOSS'S STOLEN BRIDE
by Natalie Anderson

Darcie must marry to take custody of her orphaned goddaughter, but arriving at the registry office, she finds herself without her convenient groom. Until her boss, Elias, offers a solution: he'll wed his irreplaceable assistant—immediately!

#4084 WED FOR THEIR ROYAL HEIR
Three Ruthless Kings
by Jackie Ashenden

Facing the woman he shared one reckless night with, Galen experiences the same lightning bolt of desire. Then shame at discovering the terrible mistake that tore Solace from their son. There's only one acceptable option: claiming Solace at the royal altar!

HPCNMRA0123

#4085 A CONVENIENT RING TO CLAIM HER
Four Weddings and a Baby
by Dani Collins
Life has taught orphan Quinn to trust only herself. So while her secret fling with billionaire Micah was her first taste of passion, it wasn't supposed to last forever. Dare she agree to Micah's surprising new proposition?

#4086 THE HOUSEKEEPER'S INVITATION TO ITALY
by Cathy Williams
Housekeeper Sophie is honor bound to reveal to Alessio the shocking secrets that her boss, his father, has hidden from him. Still, Sophie didn't expect Alessio to make her the solution to his family's problems...by inviting her to Lake Garda as his pretend girlfriend!

#4087 THE PRINCE'S FORBIDDEN CINDERELLA
The Secret Twin Sisters
by Kim Lawrence
Widower Prince Marco is surprised to be brought to task by his daughter's new nanny, fiery Kate! And when their forbidden connection turns to intoxicating passion, Marco finds himself dangerously close to giving in to what he's always promised to never feel...

#4088 THE NIGHTS SHE SPENT WITH THE CEO
Cape Town Tycoons
by Joss Wood
With two sisters to care for, chauffeur Lex can't risk her job. Ignoring her ridiculous attraction to CEO Cole is essential. Until a snowstorm cuts them off from reality. And makes Lex dream beyond a few forbidden nights...

YOU CAN FIND MORE INFORMATION ON UPCOMING HARLEQUIN TITLES, FREE EXCERPTS AND MORE AT HARLEQUIN.COM.

HPCNMRB0123